Beautiful Goodbye

Beautiful
Goodbye

NANCY RUNSTEDLER

DUNDURN
TORONTO

Editor: Jennifer McKnight
Design: Jennifer Scott
Printer: Webcom

Library and Archives Canada Cataloguing in Publication

Runstedler, Nancy
        Beautiful goodbye / by Nancy Runstedler.

Issued also in electronic formats.
ISBN 978-1-4597-0553-1

I. Title.

PS8635.U58B42 2013   jC813'.6   C2012-907670-8

1   2   3   4   5   17   16   15   14   13

We acknowledge the support of the Canada Council for the Arts and the Ontario Arts Council for our publishing program. We also acknowledge the financial support of the Government of Canada through the Canada Book Fund and Livres Canada Books, and the Government of Ontario through the Ontario Book Publishing Tax Credit and the Ontario Media Development Corporation.

Care has been taken to trace the ownership of copyright material used in this book. The author and the publisher welcome any information enabling them to rectify any references or credits in subsequent editions.

J. Kirk Howard, President

Printed and bound in Canada.

Visit us at
Dundurn.com
@dundurnpress
Facebook.com/dundurnpress
Pinterest.com/dundurnpress

Dundurn	Gazelle Book Services Limited	Dundurn
3 Church Street, Suite 500	White Cross Mills	2250 Military Road
Toronto, Ontario, Canada	High Town, Lancaster, England	Tonawanda, NY
M5E 1M2	LA1 4XS	U.S.A. 14150

In memory of my mother,
Margaret Evalyn Runstedler.
I miss you every day.

He spake well who said that graves are the footprints of angels.

— *Henry Wadsworth Longfellow*

When you are sorrowful look again in your heart, and you shall see that in truth you are weeping for that which has been your delight.

— *Kahlil Gibran*

Chapter One

The worn wooden planks creaked under their feet as the girls climbed the attic stairs. Maggie and Gillian yanked on the rusted door handle. On the second pull the door swung open, nearly knocking them back down the staircase. Maggie brushed aside a few cobwebs, the silken threads tangling in her hands.

"Ewww." She shuddered, struggling to swat them off. She ended up wiping the sticky strands down the legs of her jeans.

Assaulted by the stagnant air, the girls gasped and coughed. Maggie cleared her throat and stepped into the entry. The sun's morning rays filtered in through two dusty windows, lighting their way.

The stale, musty smell didn't bother Maggie. It reminded her of the stacks room at the library. The smell of books soothed her.

"I bet no one has been up here for years," Gillian said.

"Just the mice, I think," Maggie replied.

"Mice? I hate mice!" Gillian hopped around as if the

vermin had suddenly appeared, until she bumped her head on a low-hanging rafter.

"Just kidding," Maggie said, although not entirely sure there weren't any critters lurking in the shadowed corners. "I'm glad you wanted to come up here with me."

Maggie was careful not to step between the support joists. It was like walking the balance beam in gymnastics, and she'd barely passed phys. ed last term, which suited her fine, as she wasn't about to wear one of those little spandex numbers in front of anyone.

Maggie held her arms out to steady herself. She tested each step, feeling if it would support them and then motioned for Gillian to follow her lead.

Not ten feet in, Maggie stumbled.

"Watch out!" Gillian grabbed her by the sleeve just in the nick of time. A second later or an inch to the left and Maggie would have crashed through the insulation, falling to the floor below.

"Whoa. Thanks." Maggie paused for a moment, clinging to her friend until they both stopped wobbling and had regained their balance.

They kept to the beams until a solid floored hallway led them to two adjoining rooms. Maggie figured they were probably right above her brother Cole's room. She could hear the beeps from his video game through the floorboards. He was usually so wrapped up in Cosmic Avengers, he probably hadn't heard a thing. As long as he stayed down there, they were fine.

The door to the first room squeaked from their disturbance as Maggie forced it open. The girls peered inside.

"Check it out," Gillian said.

The shell of an old fireplace stood on the far wall. Several of the bricks had crumbled onto the floor, but much of it remained intact. Maggie knelt down and sifted through some rubble on the floor. Gillian used the toes of her sneakers.

"Afraid you might wreck your nails?" Maggie asked, smiling.

Gillian laughed and picked up a tin plate and cup with the tips of her fingers, as if the items were contaminated. Maggie glanced down at her own stubby nails and shrugged. She had better things to do than worry about spending time on manicures.

"I wonder who used to live here," Gillian said as she wandered back over to the fireplace, poking and feeling as if in search of a secret compartment.

"I think it was a small hotel when it was first built," Maggie replied.

After her father's sudden death, the remaining three Kaufmans had moved across town into this older, historic home in Harmony. It was all they could manage now, with just their mother's job at the travel agency, and had it not been so rundown they wouldn't have been able to afford it either.

"I miss being next door to you," Maggie said. "I might as well be on another planet." She hated all the changes. Her dad's death, the move, the start of high school — so much to adjust to at once.

Even though she drove her crazy most of the time, Maggie knew she could never have gotten through it all without her best friend.

"I hear ya," Gillian replied. "But think of the cool old stuff we might find in a house like this!" Her brilliant smile seemed to light up the place. For as long as she could remember, Maggie had been helpless to resist that grin, even when they were in first grade and it was a toothless one.

They moved into the second room and discovered a rusted metal bed frame along one wall. A small pine desk and chair sat below the solitary window. Maggie hurried over to it. She wrenched the window sash until it opened a crack, allowing some fresh fall air to enter the room. A light breeze rustled a frayed piece of newsprint on the desk she hadn't noticed at first.

"Gillian, look at this."

"I've never seen a newspaper this old before," Gillian said, as she caressed it with her French tipped fingernail.

"Me neither." It was yellowed with age, so Maggie hesitated to touch it.

Gillian leaned in and read the headline aloud.

"'Our Boys Off To War' … And look — you can still see the date at the top. *Harmony Gazette*, 1914."

Afraid it might crumble in her hands, Maggie gently slid the delicate paper into the empty desk drawer so it wouldn't blow away. She gazed out the window, deep in thought, imagining who might have lived there.

"It must have been awful to live through a war, don't you think?" she asked. Maggie knew very little about the First World War but recalled vivid details of the horrors people suffered in the Second World War from a number of books she'd read, including one of her favourites, *The Diary of Anne Frank*.

"I think it would have been kind of romantic. In the movies you always see the women tearfully waving goodbye to their men. And the soldiers always look so fine in their uniforms."

Maggie sighed. Was her friend a hopeless romantic or just hopeless? Gillian wouldn't understand. Losing someone you loved really hurt. The pain seemed unbearable at times. She lifted her locket from beneath her sweatshirt and wound the chain around her fingers. Gillian's squeal startled her.

"Now this is totally sweet!"

"What is it?" Maggie turned and asked.

"It's a Ouija board." Gillian picked up a tattered box.

"A what?"

"You know. One of those old boards that you can ask questions and it will tell you the answers," Gillian said. "I think my mom used to have one, like back in the seventies."

Maggie looked blank, which only seemed to rev Gillian up more.

"I've read stories of people contacting ghosts with these things. It was just lying here in the corner. The box is a bit beat up but I bet you the board is still okay."

"Read? Like what kind of stories?" Maggie asked.

"I *do* read, you know."

"Gillian, those trashy magazines at the grocery checkout don't count."

"Well I've seen stuff about this on talk shows too."

"So let's try it then," Maggie said.

"Are you crazy? I was thinking more like selling it on eBay and making a few bucks. But try it? What if something awful happens?"

"Like what?" Maggie asked.

"Like … like we contact the spirit of some mass murderer or something."

"Gillian, you've got to quit watching those horror flicks."

A cool chill swept through the room. Gillian hunched her chin into the warmth of her sweater but Maggie ignored it, fascinated by the board. She set the box on the floor and plopped herself down cross-legged, too excited to even worry about getting her clothes dirty.

"Chill, Gillian. It will be fun. I mean, what could possibly go wrong?"

Chapter Two

As Maggie eased the lid from the box, a moth escaped, flying haphazardly toward Gillian's face. Startled, she jumped back, hands whacking away the unwelcome insect.

Maggie stifled a giggle.

"It's not funny!" Gillian said, still swatting the air around her head.

"Sorry." Maggie removed the board from the box and began to examine it.

Goosebumps emerged on her skin, despite the heat of the attic. She rubbed her arms up and down then tucked her trembling hands under her armpits.

What's wrong with me, she thought. *There's nothing to be afraid of. But what if...? Don't even go there,* she ordered herself. *No point getting your hopes up about something that will never happen. Just have fun with it.*

Gillian joined her on the floor. The girls balanced the board so that it rested flat on their knees. Gillian sat and observed as Maggie used her sleeve to dust if off then ran her fingers over its slippery surface. The wood felt cool to her touch.

"Are you sure you want to do this?" Maggie asked. She wanted to try it more than ever but she would never force Gillian. Her eyes darted back to the box and the warning it contained. She scanned the words, butterflies pirouetting in her stomach.

"Contact may be made with spirits. Exercise caution and use at your own risk. Not recommended for young children."

"I better not look at that," Gillian said. "The warning will just freak me out."

Okay, Maggie thought. *Better get started then, before she changes her mind.*

She continued to slide her hands over the mysterious-looking board. Each of the twenty-six letters of the alphabet and the numbers from zero to nine were displayed. At the bottom of the board, the words "yes," "no," and "goodbye" were also printed.

"Maybe it will tell me if Mark is going to kiss me. Or the answers to our math test next week." Gillian grinned, her eyes twinkling with mischief.

"See, now that's a better attitude," Maggie said. She rubbed her hands together as if she just couldn't wait to dive in and get started.

"Hold on. I think we need this thingy." Gillian withdrew a tiny triangle-shaped piece of wood from the box and passed it to Maggie. It resembled a doll-house table and rested on the board on three small legs. One tip of the triangle was marked as a pointer.

Maggie set it on the board and waited for Gillian to place her fingers next to hers before they tested it out. It glided easily across the wood surface. Maggie beamed like a kid with a new toy.

"What should we ask it first?" Gillian wondered aloud.

"You mean that's all there is to it?" Maggie asked.

"Well, yeah. I think we just ask it our question and it will spell out the answer."

"Wait…. Did you hear that?" Maggie asked. Her heart rate accelerated.

"Hear what?"

"I could have sworn I heard the door at the top of the stairs squeak." Maggie gnawed on what was left of her nails, a nervous habit she'd been unable to break.

"T-t-tell me it was just the wind," Gillian said.

"Yeah, maybe you're right." Then the girls heard something else. Soft at first, then increasingly louder. "Uh, Gillian … then why do I hear tapping now?"

"Tapping?" Gillian started to squirm.

"Shh. Just listen."

Either Maggie was losing her mind or someone, or something, was definitely approaching. The mysterious tapping advanced — closer and closer. With each beat, she felt a vibration shudder through the old floor boards and into her body. She trembled, spun around, and shouted, "Who's there?"

Silence.

"Maybe you should go take a look in the hall," Gillian whispered.

"Me! Why me?" Maggie hissed.

"Well, then maybe we could look together?"

Maggie glared at her but nodded. The girls set the board down and inched their way toward the hallway door, tiptoeing so as not to make a sound. All she could hear now was the rapid beating of her own heart, thudding in her ears.

Maggie snuck a look around the doorway, half expecting

someone or something to jump out at them. Gillian stayed behind her, clutching her around the waist, peeking one eye around Maggie's shoulder.

The hallway was deserted. *Could I have imagined the noise?* Maggie wondered. But Gillian had heard it too, hadn't she? "Nothing there," Maggie said.

Gillian released her death grip on Maggie's clothes and the girls turned back into the room.

"Come on," Maggie continued. "Let's try again. It's gonna be great."

Gillian sulked back to their place on the floor. Maggie knew that she could wear down Gillian's reservations. Like the first time she'd talked her into camping out in a tent in the backyard. Gillian had refused to turn her flashlight off all night, but admittedly had a blast, and now it was a ritual between them every summer.

Neither of them spoke as they repositioned the board and pointer. The girls remained on high alert. Maggie strained to hear any sound that might not be coming from them. She wiped her sweaty hands on her jeans before placing them next to Gillian's on the pointer.

"Now, where were we?" Maggie asked.

"Deciding what to ask it first," Gillian replied. "Hey. Maybe it was just the old boards creaking, eh Maggie?"

"No one has been up here in a long time. And old houses do that." *Unless there's a spirit here with us already*, Maggie thought.

Then she heard it. Not tapping this time. Maggie could hear breathing. She glanced over at Gillian. Her friend's body frozen and her mouth sealed shut, till she choked out, "M-M-Maggie?"

Maggie didn't think it was her own panting making the sound, as she drew in a lungful of air. Maybe if she held her breath she'd be able to hear if there was someone else breathing with them. Then again, her blood was pounding so hard in her ears now she realized she'd never be able to tell the difference.

Maggie squeezed her eyes closed and recoiled from the noise. The bitter taste of fear filled her mouth. Gillian wasn't the only one scared now.

The sound was getting louder and closer. It was right behind her.

Chapter Three

Fingernails gripped Maggie's shoulders like claws.

"Ahhh!" she screamed.

Gillian started to laugh. And laugh some more. *What in the world could possibly be so funny at a time like this?* Maggie wondered. She opened her eyes just enough to peek out a thin slit.

The hands on her shoulders looked very familiar.

"Cole!" Maggie shrieked. "What are you doing here?"

"I followed you," he said as she swatted him in the arm. "Ouch! I could hear someone walking around above my room."

"And you'll follow those stairs right back down." She so sounded like her mother now. She whacked him again, but without much force behind it.

"Nope. This is way more exciting than video games." A sly grin spread across his face as he held up his arms in protection from further blows.

"You should have seen the look on your face," Gillian said. She wiped tears of glee from her cheeks. "Priceless."

"Like you weren't scared too." *This is just great*, thought Maggie. *Just what I don't need.* "Cole, I'm not asking you — I'm telling you."

"Deal with it, freckle face. I don't want to be stuck here with you today either, but if you don't let me stay, I'll tell Mom."

Maggie sighed. She couldn't believe she was going to concede defeat. Thankfully it would only be a couple more years before he could fend for himself and her babysitting days would be over.

"All right, but don't you dare tell Mom. And don't touch the board. You can sit in the corner and watch."

"Deal." Cole plopped himself down out of the girls' way.

"I'm so glad I'm an only child," Gillian giggled.

"Okay, let's get started," Maggie said. "I'll ask the questions." Knowing Gillian, she'd ask something Maggie didn't want Cole knowing about.

Once again, the girls rested their fingertips on either side of the pointer. Maggie was careful not to add any unnecessary weight or pressure with her hands. She looked at Gillian with a reassuring smile.

Maggie slowly asked, "How old am I?"

They could do this. It would be fun. Just like camping.

At first nothing happened. Maggie tried to release the tension in her body. She eased her neck around in a circle, stretching her stiff muscles and wiggling her shoulders.

They tried again.

Still the pointer didn't stir.

"Relax," she said and motioned for Gillian to mimic her techniques.

The girls did a few more moves to loosen up then placed their fingers back on the pointer. Again, it didn't budge.

"What's wrong with this thing?" Maggie said as she picked the pointer up, gave it a shake, and then put it back on the board. She shrugged at the others when they looked at her as if she were crazy.

"Maybe it's not moving because someone in the room doesn't believe," Gillian threw out for consideration.

"Cole?" Maggie eyeballed him but he shook his head. She knew she wanted this to work out more than anything. One look at Gillian and Maggie knew her friend was in no state to question matters. "How old am I?" She asked once more.

Gradually it started to move. *Yes!* Maggie thought.

It jerked to the left and stopped at the one, as if an invisible force had moved it. She glanced across at Gillian to see her shocked face. The pointer began to move again. This time its journey on the board led it to the four.

Fourteen.

"Unbelievable!" Maggie said. "Let's do it again."

"Are you sure you're not cheating?" Gillian asked. "Someone always cheats … don't they?"

Maggie knew she wasn't pushing the pointer. This had to be legit. "No!" At Gillian's doubtful stare, she continued. "Honest."

"Then close your eyes this time so you can't see where the pointer is going."

"Will you believe me then?" Maggie asked.

"Just do it."

Maggie realized she needed to pose a question that neither of them knew the answer to. Only then would they have the proof to know it was truly happening.

"What colour is Cole's underwear?"

"Gross," Gillian said.

Cole snorted from the corner.

This time the pointer started to slowly circle the board, landing on letters. Maggie kept her eyes firmly shut till the others gave the okay.

"Purple?" Gillian winced.

Cole laughed and peeled the top of his baggy jeans back just enough to reveal that the board was indeed correct.

"I think I'll be the one to close my eyes from now on," Gillian said.

Maggie didn't move a muscle. There was no way Gillian could have known that. How many people actually wear purple underwear? She hadn't known it either.

There was something incredibly mysterious about this board. A mixture of trepidation and curiosity battled within her. If it could answer these simple questions, maybe, just maybe, it could do more.

Maggie yearned to ask it something about her father but didn't dare in front of Cole. She needed to find a way to get rid of him so the girls could continue alone. "Maybe we should quit while we're ahead."

"Are you kidding? This is actually sort of fun," Gillian said.

"Yeah!" Cole agreed.

"Okay. Okay. One more." So much for that idea.

Maggie's eyes wandered around the room in silent awe. What had happened inside this house? She'd felt drawn to the newspaper article the girls had discovered and wondered who it belonged to. She had no idea what it must have been like to live here when it was first built. If only these walls could talk.

Maggie took a deep breath, the words out of her mouth before she could stop herself. "Is anyone here with us?"

Maggie willed herself to remain still and concentrate. Nothing happened. She repeated her question then glanced at her brother and friend but their eyes seemed glued to the board. *Focus*, she thought.

Little by little the pointer started to move. It settled on the word …

YES

"We did it!" Maggie cheered then stopped herself. Unless we haven't contacted who I meant to, she thought, now imagining the worst. But there wasn't time to think and it was too late to turn back without looking like a wimp.

"Who are you?" she asked instead.

All of a sudden, the pointer increased its pace and began to skim the surface, faster and faster. Maggie felt powerless to stop it. She dared not look away for even a second, should she miss one of the letters. It slipped from one to the next, building into a frenzy, then coming to a sudden halt at the centre of the board.

No one spoke a word. There were a lot of letters to follow; requiring every ounce of their concentration, but the communication had come through.

The message simply said:

```
My name is Hope Lewis. Once I lived
and loved. I am here with you now.
```

Chapter Four

"Girl, I th-th-think your house is haunted," Gillian said.

"Everyone knows there's no such thing as ghosts," Cole scoffed, though he was unable to hide the tremor in his voice. "It's lunchtime anyway. I'm outta here."

Great. How can he even think about eating at a time like this, Maggie wondered. "Come on, Gillian. If I don't feed him right away, he'll tell my mom I withheld food."

"Gee, just when it was getting exciting too," Gillian said.

For someone so interested, Maggie thought her friend couldn't follow Cole's lead fast enough. Why was she the only one who didn't want to stop?

"You okay?" Gillian asked as they headed downstairs, although Maggie thought her friend looked a little shaky herself.

She nodded. As freaky as it might seem to the others, she was dying to know more. It wasn't like the spirit had been evil. If anything, it was probably just lonely since the house had been empty for a while before they moved in. And Maggie knew loneliness well.

She clenched her hands at her sides and thought about the day the moving van had arrived. Since then, she'd refused to finish unpacking, though they'd been here for two months now and it was obvious, even to her, that they weren't going back. She'd yet to hang up any of her posters and even all of her favourite books sat in boxes, the cardboard cubes lined against the wall in front of lonely shelves.

Back in the kitchen, no one spoke as Maggie popped a frozen pizza into the oven for lunch. *How odd for Gillian not to have anything to say*, she thought. Even Cole wasn't hollering about how long till his food was ready.

As soon as the timer beeped, Maggie barely had Cole's slices onto a plate before he dove in. Gillian grabbed the juice from the fridge and poured them each a glass.

Maggie picked at her pepperoni. With her mom working yet another Saturday, Maggie was in charge. She didn't recognize herself or her family these days. Part of her felt like her mom was never home anymore. Before her dad died, her mom used to be such a homebody, greeting them with freshly baked oatmeal cookies after a day at school and planning family outings for the weekends. Corny maybe, but she missed those things.

Maggie had watched her leave earlier this morning from the entry to the kitchen, her body half hidden behind the doorframe, as her mother kissed Cole goodbye.

"Thanks for holding the fort again today, sweetheart," her mother said.

"Whatever," she mumbled and turned to walk away.

"Maggie dear, I wish you would talk to me. Or someone."

Maggie didn't want to talk. She felt like a good chunk of her had died along with her father. She was just fine, thank you very much, with the numbness that had settled into every pore of her body. Okay, well maybe not fine, as Maggie knew full well she was in denial. But numb was the only sensation, or lack thereof, that she could handle. If she let herself feel anything more, she would crumble. And all the king's horses and all the king's men would never be able to put her back together again.

"Sweetie, you know I have no choice but to go to work. You know I'd much rather be here with you guys. Please don't do this." Her mother sighed. "I need to go or I'll be late."

Maggie watched her mother jam her keys in her purse, ruffle Cole's shaggy mop of hair, and blow them both a kiss as she hurried out the back door.

Maggie envisioned other girls her age, romping through the mall, searching for the perfect outfit, giggling and flirting with boys as they swung their bags. Not stuck with their ten-year-old brothers.

"Yo, sis!" Cole said.

"Huh?" She shook her head to find the others gawking at her. What had she missed?

"You wanna go back up, don't you?" Gillian asked.

"Yup." No question about it. Maggie's slice of pizza sat untouched but the others' plates were empty.

Every time she'd passed the door leading up to the attic, she'd paused, her curiosity piqued. With helping her mother unpack, babysitting, and starting school, there just hadn't been time. 'Till now. This was even better than her old *Nancy Drew* mysteries, and it was happening to her. She just *had* to find out more.

She cleared her plate, scooped their lunch dishes into the sink, and turned to the others.

"Let's do it."

Maggie dashed upstairs, her footsteps echoing behind her, the others trailing behind. The girls barely had their fingers back on the pointer when it started to move again, as if the spirit had been waiting for their return. Their hands moved as if they were puppets on an invisible string. The kids read aloud as the words took shape.

```
Fear not. Please do not go.
```

The only thing Maggie was afraid of at this point was not finding out more. Once again the words slipped from her mouth. "When did you die?"

Gillian raised her eyebrows in alarm, her fingers still firmly placed on the pointer. Maggie felt bolder by the minute. Cole remained rapt and edged his way in from the corner. They did not wait long for their next message.

```
I lived from 1898 to 1988.
```

"Wow she's old!" Cole said.

"Shhh." Maggie glared at him. She was pretty certain about the next answer but had to know for sure.

"Where did you live?"

```
This was my home.
```

Maggie had suspected as much and disconnected her hands from the board. This was really getting close to home now. Maybe too close. It was one thing to throw herself into the unknown but she couldn't force the others.

"From now on we do all of our sleepovers at my house," Gillian said. "No way am I climbing into bed with some ghost roaming about!"

"Gillian!" Maggie made eye contact with her friend and then motioned with her head in Cole's direction. "Some of us have to live here, you know. I think we'd better pack it up."

"Just sayin'," Gillian said.

Maggie shook her head to clear the eerie images forming in her brain. That wasn't how she wanted to think of this spirit. She had a name, and Hope sounded anything but bad.

The girls put the board back in its box and set it on the bed frame. Cole high-tailed it down the stairs with Gillian at his heels. Maggie turned to close the attic door and paused, a sudden sadness tugging at her heart. She glanced back over her shoulder one last time then headed back to the kitchen.

Chapter Five

"Maybe she was totally rich and owned the hotel," Gillian said. "I can just picture her with a flowing emerald evening gown and long white gloves, greeting her guests."

Maggie's eyebrows shot up. "What?" She paced back and forth over the worn linoleum floor. She wondered if her feet were treading in the same spot as Hope's once had.

"Her hair as dark as night, cascading down her back," Gillian continued, staring into space.

"Which would describe you to a tee if you hadn't chopped yours off into that spiky style you have now."

"I thought you liked my new look." Gillian pouted, pretending to be hurt. "On second thought, maybe she wore it up in a twist with a fancy clip, a few tendrils elegantly escaping."

"This is serious, Gillian." Maggie tapped her fingers nervously on the kitchen counter. "We need to find out if this … this person was real. If she was, I need to know what happened to her."

"Why?" Cole asked.

"What do you mean, why?" Maggie couldn't imagine stopping now.

"Why do *we* have to be the ones to figure this all out?"

"Because …" she hesitated. "Because even though I don't like it, this is our home now. I need to know what happened here. Besides, people will think we're crazy if we tell anyone else about it."

"He's got a point, though," Gillian said. "Maybe we should just let it go."

"Fine. I'll do it myself then if you guys are too chicken!"

"Wait, Maggie," Gillian said.

"Maybe Miss Menkle at the library can help," Cole offered. "You always used to hang out there."

"You're right. I knew I kept you around for something." Maggie grabbed their jackets from the hook at the kitchen's back door.

"We're going to the library on a Saturday?" Gillian protested.

They walked the few short blocks to Harmony's Carnegie Library. Cole wandered ahead of the two girls. He kicked at the piles of leaves collecting under the giant maples that lined the wide streets, their yellows, oranges, and reds like flames leaping in the air. The girls couldn't leave him at home alone, especially with a spirit in residence.

Maggie cautioned Gillian about what to say once they reached the library.

"We can't let Miss Menkle know what we're really up to. It's a small town and the gossip will spread faster than your phone number in the boys' locker room if anyone finds out about Hope."

"Why don't we pretend you're searching for a lost relative?" Gillian suggested, ignoring the stinging remark.

"Great idea." Maggie instantly felt sorry for her comment, but it was too late to take it back. She knew she'd been angry a lot lately and that Gillian had been one of the people to suffer from her verbal blows.

They walked up the steps into the red brick building and went straight to the main desk. Miss Menkle greeted them with a smile and did not seem suspicious at all when they asked for her help.

She'd dressed casually for her weekend shift, wearing bell-bottom jeans, a flowered blouse, dangly earrings, and her long hair tied back in a braid.

"Is the hippie look back in?" Gillian whispered.

Thankfully, Maggie didn't figure Miss Menkle heard, as she was too busy winking at Cole, who still had some leaves stuck in his hair. He blushed profusely, his dimples showing.

She led them proudly over to the local history section, her eagerness contagious, and began pulling out volumes for them to look through. One after another, she piled the reference books up on a large wooden work table. The trio grabbed chairs and sat around, ready to begin.

"With a date of birth and death, as well as both first and last names, you kids shouldn't have any trouble finding what you need," Miss Menkle said. "And it's good to see you, Maggie. I've missed our chats. You know there are lots of new titles in the young adult section if you want to have a look."

"Thanks," Maggie said, avoiding direct eye contact, "but this is all for today." Maggie missed coming here too.

She'd never dreamt in her worst nightmares that she'd ever stop reading. It was almost like giving up breathing. But she just couldn't seem to concentrate on anything since her dad died. Every time she tried, the words became a blur of tears.

"Well just let me know if you need anything else then." With that, the librarian strode back to the circulation desk.

Gillian stumbled across the first bit of information. She held up some county records and waved them in the air. "Hey! It says here your house was built in 1868."

"Let's see." Maggie scooted over to her.

"And the first owner's last name was Morris, and the second last name, Lewis."

"Way to go!" Maggie held up her hand and the girls touched the knuckles of their fists together.

After that it was slow going. Cole sat chewing on his gum, the snaps of breaking bubbles irritating his sister. She stared at him until he caught the hint and stopped. He asked to go use the computer internet stations available to the public, but she refused, wanting them to stick close together. He could help out too, she thought. Cole stayed but resumed his gum chomping in defiance.

Gillian picked at her nails, her eyes now glazed over. Maggie rubbed the kink in her neck but kept searching to find some answers. She rummaged around for what felt like hours and now held up a huge volume with a look of triumph on her face. Cole elbowed Gillian then looked to his sister with interest.

"What did you find?" he asked.

"Census records."

"Cen ... who?" Gillian asked.

"Census records. It's how the population is counted. It lists the number of people in each home and their names." Maggie dropped the heavy book with a thud, nearly crushing her finger that held her place.

"Ouch!" She lowered her voice. "And look near the bottom of this page. Here's the last name Lewis and a listing of family members. Hope's name is right here, as well as three brothers and her parents!"

"Now we're getting somewhere," Gillian said as she rubbed her eyes and sat up straight.

"I can't believe we found it," Maggie said. Excitement surged through her veins. It felt good to be enthused about something again.

"This is, like, sooo eerie," Gillian said.

I won't let Gillian spoil this for me, Maggie thought.

"Anything else?" Cole asked.

"Nope. That's as far as it goes." Maggie jotted the new information down on a scrap of paper and said, "But what we really need is more proof of Hope's death. No way am I going through that huge stack of death records or blinding my eyes on microfiche. I hate to say this, but I think we should head over to the cemetery."

"Cemetery!" Gillian cried. "I really should be getting home...."

"No lame excuses," Maggie said.

Cole shuffled nervously. "Yeah, if I gotta go along, so do you."

Gillian hung her head and sighed.

Maggie tidied the papers and reference books. "I need you to stick with me on this. You're my best friend. Besides, don't you want to find out if this is all for real?"

Gillian cringed and gave Maggie a sheepish smile. "Let's hurry before it gets late. Cemeteries are even creepier in the dark."

Chapter Six

The kids thanked Miss Menkle and strode down the block. They continued on Queen Street, past the butcher, grocery store, bank, and flower shop. Gillian smiled in the windows of Clip N' Curl as they passed. One stylist waved back with her free hand as she brushed and blow dried.

Soon the familiar old sign for Woodland Cemetery came into view. Over the years the sign had started to hang crooked, but no one seemed bothered enough by it to fix it. The cemetery bordered on the edge of town and backed onto forested land. Some sections of it dated back hundreds of years.

As they entered and veered around newly dug plots, the scent of freshly turned earth filled Maggie's nostrils. While others thought of that smell as new life in spring or the sign of fall's harvest, to her it symbolized only death. She wouldn't even consider the fact that her dad was under that earth, yet somehow being here helped her to feel closer to him. That alone erased any fear for her. She worried about her brother though, since this had to be his first time back to the cemetery since their dad's funeral. Maybe she should have insisted he stay at home. To Maggie's relief, no one else appeared to be around.

"There must be hundreds of headstones. Which way should we go?" Cole asked.

"We could each take a section," Maggie suggested, checking once again to see that he was okay.

Gillian grabbed her hand and held tight. "There's no way we're splitting up."

"Then we'd better get started." Maggie dragged her friend along. Even though he could be a royal pain, she really didn't want to upset Cole, so she avoided the area where their father was buried and instead led them off in the other direction.

She hadn't told anyone about her private visits to the cemetery. Maggie didn't know if she would ever be able to talk about them. She swallowed hard but couldn't dislodge the lump in her throat.

They soon entered an area where the inscriptions had faded over time, making them difficult to read. Some of the old white stones were starting to tip over, slanting and losing their grip in the earth. Maggie sighed softly as her eyes swept over the rows of lonely headstones that no one seemed to visit anymore. But then maybe there was no one left alive to come and visit those ones. At least this part of the cemetery lacked any current signs of remembrance, such as the flowers she tended in front of her father's stone. Even the grass seemed longer and neglected. Maggie vowed never to let that happen to her father's grave.

Gillian seemed to be holding up okay but was never more than a few feet away. Cole, on the other hand, ventured ahead of the girls, his earlier hesitation apparently replaced with a new sense of adventure. He jumped over each grave then stopped to peer at the inscriptions. It was a far cry from the little boy who'd stood frozen in grief a few months earlier.

The girls carefully made their way up and down the paths, speaking in hushed tones. Maggie shook her head, thinking nobody could hear them anyway. Row by row they went, working their way through. Many times she had to lean in close to read the worn lettering. Her heart felt heavy every time she passed a stone where a life had been cut too short. She looked over at Gillian who was kneeling in front of a grave a few stones down the row, and headed over toward her.

"I think I found something," Gillian said.

Maggie bent down to have a closer look.

"Boo!" Cole shouted and jumped out from behind the stone. Gillian and Maggie fell backwards into the grass, grabbing each other for dear life.

They looked up at Cole standing over them, laughing like crazy, and jumped back up. "You little twerp!" Maggie said. "Don't you ever do that again!" She couldn't believe that she'd wasted her time ever worrying about bringing him here.

Gillian moved back to the stone, her hands still visibly shaking from Cole's prank. She gently dusted some dirt and dried leaves off the surface with her palm. "Yup. This one is for an Edward Lewis."

Cole quit laughing and joined the girls, oddly serious now, even for him.

"Born 1873 and died 1915. Loving father and husband," Maggie read. It matched the name for Hope's father. It seemed he had died young as well. Add the fact that they'd both lived in the same house, and the similarities were starting to add up.

The trio looked to the next grave. The headstone was much newer and clearer to read. It belonged to Hope's mother, who had thankfully lived a longer life. The next three stones' names corresponded with those they'd discovered to be Hope's brothers. So far it appeared that there wasn't anyone left living in the family.

After a few moments of shared silence, their gaze rested on the last and newest grave.

Hope Evalyn Lewis
1898–1988
Mother, Daughter, and Friend.

Rest in Peace

Maggie's breath caught. *My goodness, it's really true*, she thought. The pieces were coming together.

She noticed Gillian had leaned closer, as if she couldn't believe what she was seeing either. Even Cole seemed affected and stood solemnly, his shoulders hunched.

"Well, the good news is that we now have proof," Maggie said. "Hope was … is for real."

"A ghost living in your house is a good thing?" Gillian asked.

"Who says all ghosts are scary? What about Casper the Friendly Ghost? And anyway, I prefer to think of her as a spirit."

"Cartoon hour is over, Maggie. And why is her spirit still hanging around your attic?"

"I wish I knew. There must be something holding her back. If we could figure out what is was, maybe she could finally move on." Maggie wondered now if other spirits were lurking around in limbo. She had no idea how it all really worked.

"Come on, sis. Get serious," Cole said.

"I am!" Maggie didn't know what she believed anymore. But she *did* know that they had to use the Ouija board again. Soon.

According to the headstone, Hope had married, borne children, and lived a long life. But new questions popped up. Had Hope been happy? How did she die? And why on earth had she contacted Maggie from beyond?

The late day sun warmed their backs, changing the shadows around them.

"We'd better get home and start supper before Mom gets back," Maggie said.

"Lead the way." Gillian followed the siblings down the path.

When they reached the main intersection of town, Maggie turned. "Thanks, Gillian."

"I really wasn't that scared, you know."

"I know." Maggie smiled at her. "So it won't be a problem for you to use the board again then?"

"I knew you were going to say that." Gillian flung her hands in the air and groaned. "When?"

"Mom's home all day tomorrow and I don't want her to catch us. How about right after school on Monday? We'll have a couple of hours before she gets home from work."

Gillian nodded and waved. Maggie turned to Cole and they set out in the direction of their street.

"You don't breathe a word of this to Mom, right?" Maggie stared down at her brother.

"Geez, I know. I got it the first time."

After that, the two barely exchanged a word. Cole grabbed a stick and dragged it along the sidewalk. Maggie paced her steps to avoid walking on the cracks, lost in thought.

It could have been just a coincidence that they'd discovered the Ouija board. Then again, maybe it was fate. Maggie sensed Hope's spirit had come to them for a reason, and knew she wouldn't be able to stop until she found out why.

Chapter Seven

On Saturday night Maggie tossed and turned, staring at her ceiling. She concentrated on trying to feel Hope's presence, but any sense of calm eluded her. Punching her pillow, she flopped over again, her blankets a tangled mess.

She needed to do something … anything … but she'd promised the others she would wait till Monday. The red digits on her alarm clock clicked past, one after another.

The Kaufmans spent a quiet day together on Sunday. Together, in the sense that they were all home at the same time. Mother and son used part of the afternoon to carve pumpkins and sip hot cider by the fireplace. Maggie listened to Cole's howls of delight as he spent hours perfecting his ghoulish jack-o-lantern.

Maggie sat slumped in what she still considered her dad's favourite armchair. The burgundy leather had faded and cracked in spots but she was grateful that her mother had moved it with them. There'd been countless arguments, albeit harmless ones, between her parents about getting rid of that "ugly old thing."

"Come help us out, sweetie," her mother said.

Maggie shook her head and stared out the window. She squeezed her worn copy of *Charlotte's Web* to her chest. While she hadn't been able to open the familiar pages yet, she'd at least pulled it out of the packing boxes. Some people had comfort food. Maggie had comfort books.

It was the first novel she'd read on her own and she'd lost count of how many nights she'd curled up beside her father in this very chair to share their cherished book.

A tear slid down her cheek as she recalled resting her head on his shoulder as he imitated the animals' voices. She loved his rendition of the goo-goo-goose the best. He'd even started calling her "some kid," her pet nickname right up until he died. They'd moved on to more complex novels over the years but their closeness and love of literature had never waned. Maggie clung to the chair like a lifeboat, washed away in a sea of grief, the waves of despair slamming the shores of her heart.

The day crept along in a blur of bittersweet memories.

On Sunday night, Cole snuck into her room.

"Do we really have to do this tomorrow?" he whispered.

"Well I am." Maggie sat up in her bed. "But if you're too scared, you can wimp out. In fact, I should never have let you become involved in this in the first place. Just please don't tell anyone."

"My silence could cost you, ya know?"

"How much?" she sighed.

"You still owe me five bucks from the last time I covered for you, so …"

"You mean blackmailed me."

"I'm your brother. I would never do such a thing."

Maggie rolled her eyes. "How much?" she asked again.

"Nah … I'm still in." Cole puffed out his chest, all bravado. "I'd rather watch Gillian freak out than take your money anyway." As he reached the door, he added, "Besides, you might just need me."

On Monday, pummelled by a downpour that soaked through to their skin from the dash between the bus stop and the back door, Maggie and Cole peeled off their school clothes. They changed and she tossed their sopping wet things into the dryer.

Rain pelted the windows and thunder boomed throughout the old walls. The lights flickered but somehow managed to stay on. Maggie heard the back door slam and nearly jumped out of her sneakers. She went to see if the wind had blown it open.

Gillian stood there and shook herself off like a dog, spraying them both and leaving a puddle on the floor. Maggie grabbed some towels and offered one as she mopped up the water.

"It's wicked out there," Gillian said. "You *had* to move to the other side of town, didn't you?" She'd used the towel to wrap her head and had traces of mascara down her cheeks.

The girls ran up to Maggie's bedroom. Maggie searched around in her dresser drawers and lent her friend a tracksuit. They were about the same height but Gillian's curves filled out the fabric better than Maggie's boyish figure ever could. Maggie didn't care. She'd always been the tomboy of the two, with the only man in her life being her dad.

After adding Gillian's wet items to the tumbling dryer, they returned to the kitchen to put the kettle on. Once the water boiled, she handed Gillian a steaming cup of hot chocolate.

"Are you ready?" Maggie asked, warming her hands on her mug.

"Ready as I'll ever be, I guess." Gillian shrugged. "I mean I did get us into this whole mess in the first place by finding the board."

"But I'm the one who made us use it," she said.

"I'm sorry for complaining the other day, Maggie. I think I understand why you're doing this."

"You do?"

"You miss your dad."

Maggie gulped. Could Gillian really see through her that well? She wanted to talk to Gillian about her father's death, but each time she tried, the words got stuck in her throat. Gillian still had both of her parents. How could she possibly understand?

Cole bounded into the room carrying a flashlight. "We might need this," he said. He'd brought a notebook and pencil with him. "And I'll write down whatever Hope tells you. It will be easier to follow along for the long messages."

Maggie glanced at the clock as the three turned to go upstairs. Four o'clock. Her mom would be home by six. Time to get started.

- - -

Once more, the wood planks groaned underfoot. Maggie held the old spindle railing for support. Wedged between the others, Gillian clung to Maggie's belt as they ventured up each step. The door at the top of the stairs opened easier than before.

They took a short walk over the beams again and everything appeared to be as they'd left it — two small attic rooms, forgotten in time, their layers of dust undisturbed except for where the trio had left their mark. The wait to come back up here had seemed interminable to Maggie.

This time, the weather cast a gloomy pall over the walls. The sky had turned a deep shade of purple and the occasional flash of lightning provided the only light. When Cole turned on the flashlight, its faint yellowish beam sliced through the shadows.

No one attempted to speak over the resounding booms and cracks of the storm as they set up the Ouija board and seated themselves around it.

"Hey, it says here on the box that this pointer thing is called a *planchette*," Maggie said.

"Cool," Gillian replied, "French always sounds so much more exotic."

Maggie still refused to let Cole touch the board, and tapped his hand away when he tried. He scribbled a few swirls on the notepad, some not very flattering caricatures of the girls, and grumbled something she couldn't make out.

Gillian looked across to her, offered an encouraging smile, and placed her fingers on the planchette.

Maggie took a deep breath and followed suit. "Are you with us, Hope?" she asked.

Branches of an ancient oak scratched at the window pane as the wind picked up outside. The rain continued its fierce attack.

The pointer moved.

YES

Thank goodness, Maggie thought. She'd been worried that by waiting, that Hope might not come back. She couldn't wait to find out more about her. Maggie's heart started to thump so hard she thought it would burst out of her chest. Gillian nodded for her to continue.

"Why are you here?"

Again the pointer began to stir. Cole scribbled furiously to keep up. Maggie let the magic of the board take over her movements, her arms swaying back and forth between letters till the rhythm became so gentle it was almost soothing. When the planchette finished, Cole read out the message.

I need your help.

"What can *we* do?" Gillian blurted. "We're just a bunch of kids!" The board lay still. They waited for a few moments, but nothing happened.

"I guess you're the only one she'll talk to," Gillian said.

Maggie sensed she was right. Somehow, a connection was forming between her and Hope. *Give me a sign*, she thought. *Just tell me what you need from us.*

Before she had a chance to voice her feelings, the planchette circled the board. It was as if Hope had connected to her thoughts. She flinched as the thunder cracked again and the window pane trembled.

The planchette's speed increased with the intensity of the storm outside. Maggie's fingers cramped as she struggled to maintain her grip, the ebb and flow movements now replaced with a greater urgency. The planchette launched itself across the slick wood with quick, lurching movements.

"What's happening?" Gillian yelled over the noise of the wind.

"I don't know!" Maggie shouted back over the din.

The flashlight dimmed. Cole gave it a shake. It faltered again and then went out completely.

"Maggie!" Gillian hollered. "I can't let go."

Cole grabbed onto his sister's leg as her arms jerked and fingers flew. Maggie felt powerless to stop Hope's spirit. It was as if an invisible force was sucking them in.

The board began rising off the floor, the kids hovering with it.

A tingling sensation swept throughout Maggie's entire being and her body felt light, then completely weightless, as if she were floating. A beam of light, like a ray of fire, shot out of the centre of the board. Brighter and brighter it grew until it became too painful for Maggie to look at it. She closed her eyes and hung on tight.

"Ahhhh!" they screamed, but their cries were lost in the thunder.

Chapter Eight

Warmth spread through Maggie, transforming her fear into a feeling of peacefulness. Before she knew it, the board landed with a crash, sending the planchette flying across the room. The trio collapsed in a heap.

Almost disappointed that it was over, she opened her eyes, rubbed them to clear her confusion, and then looked again.

"You guys okay?" She asked.

Cole and Gillian nodded but didn't move. Maggie eased herself into a standing position, her legs a bit shaky but otherwise unharmed. She blinked several times.

They hadn't gone anywhere, but the attic room looked different. Maggie could smell wood smoke. She turned to see a fire blazing in the hearth that moments ago lay crumbled. A thin mattress and old woolen blankets covered the bed frame. The desk still stood in the corner below the window, though an unlit lantern and a frayed book, left open, now sat on it.

A black steamer trunk leaned open against the wall. *That*

wasn't there before either, she thought. The room was clean and dust free now, but still sparsely furnished.

Gillian found her voice. "What on earth …"

"*Shh*. Listen," Maggie said.

The sound of music and people's voices drifted up from the floors below. Doors clunked open and closed. Maggie felt the hairs on the back of her neck stand at attention. Gillian panted in short sharp breaths, about to hyperventilate till Maggie eased her friend's head between her knees.

Just as she was sure Gillian was no longer at risk of passing out, she saw Cole head for the door.

Before Maggie could stop him, he crept down the rickety stairs. The girls followed just in time to see him peek out of the attic entrance into the hallway. As quick as the lightning outside, he jerked his head back in.

"The hall's full of people carrying suitcases and wearing funny old clothes!"

Maggie and Gillian pushed past him. Sure enough, they watched as a woman guided two small girls and entered a doorway down the hall.

"That's my room!" Maggie whispered.

The children wore matching dresses with lace cuffs, full enough to indicate petticoats underneath, their braided hair tied with pink ribbon. The woman, who Maggie assumed to be their mother, had buttoned her collared blouse up to her neck and the hemline of her long grey skirt only missed skimming the floor by a few inches.

A girl appearing slightly older than Maggie and Gillian walked silently behind the mother and daughters, carrying their luggage. A few tendrils of pale blond hair escaped from her bun. Her faded brown dress looked like a potato sack in comparison to the garments of those with her, but did nothing to diminish her beauty.

"What's going on?" Gillian, still pale, ducked back behind the doorframe, leaving only her eyes peeking out.

Two men in brown wool soldiers' uniforms hurried down the hall with an air of purpose. The heels of their polished boots echoed behind them on the floor boards.

"I'd say they were just into vintage, but that doesn't explain the guys' army duds," Gillian continued in a whisper.

It doesn't make any sense, Maggie thought. *What's happened to our house?*

"Maybe they're all ghosts," Cole said.

"Not more ghosts!" Gillian closed her eyes and hid her head in her hands.

Maggie could only see one answer. Somehow, it seemed they had travelled back in time. But no, that couldn't be possible, and yet.... She rubbed her forehead. She still felt a bit fuzzy.

"Hope must have brought us here." Maggie tried to deal with the facts in front of them. "They're as real as we are, so we can't let anyone see us."

"Why not?" Gillian asked. "I'd love to ask the mother where she got that outfit."

Good grief, Maggie thought. *You and your one-track mind.* But Maggie *did* need to warn them. "Because we'll stick out like sore thumbs. We can't just tell people that we came here from the future because a spirit dragged us through a Ouija board!"

"Oh man. Mom's gonna freak," Cole said.

"Come on. And be quiet!" She grabbed her brother and friend and hurried back up to the relative safety of the attic.

Her brother was right. If Maggie didn't find a way to sort this all out and have her brother back home in one piece before her mom got off work she'd be grounded for the rest of her life.

"We need a plan," she said. "But first we should have a look around."

Maggie paced back and forth in the tiny room while Cole busied himself with putting the board and its parts back in the box and under the bed. Before she knew it he was in front of the fireplace, poking at logs, sparks flying every which way.

"Can you not touch anything?" she said. "I need to think!" She pulled the poker out of his hand and scooped the fallen ash up with a small metal shovel.

Maggie struggled to keep control. Where would they get the clothes to make them fit in enough to avoid suspicion? She wrung her hands, feeling sick at the predicament they were in. They couldn't stay here like this. Sooner or later they would be discovered and she had no idea how they would explain it. And if they didn't get out of here, how would she ever justify this harebrained adventure to her mom? On the other hand, if they never saw her mom again, there'd be no need to explain anything.

"Why would Hope have done this?" Maggie cried. More importantly, how would they ever get back to the home they knew? Her head reeled. She continued to pace.

"Let's not panic. This could be fun," Gillian said.

Hadn't Maggie used these exact same words before? Her steps led her to the desk and she looked down at a worn journal. She skimmed a few pages, gently turning the paper, and then stopped at the latest entry.

October 18, 1915

Dear Diary,

Mama came to visit today. I've missed her terribly. She was on her way into the city to look for work at the ammunitions factory. She's finding it difficult without Pa and Luke. I pray every day that they're safe. Men are hurrying off to fight in what they're calling the "Great War," thinking it will make them heroes, but I believe they're wrong. What is so "great" about any war? What good can come of any death?

I keep these thoughts to myself, however, as most people seem to disagree. I know Adam feels like a failure that he was unable to enlist because of his flat feet, but I see it as a blessing. He will be able to stay here and help Mama with Max and the farm.

Other girls are talking about joining the Nursing Sisters but I need to stay here right now. I'm glad that I am able to send home a bit of money from my job in the hotel, but my hands ache from all the scrubbing and I am lonely. I will do my best to stay strong. I've not heard from Franz in several days and I am really worried. Please God, let him be safe. I love him so.

Maggie knew in a moment that the diary must be Hope's. So this had to be her room. *Yes! Now maybe we're getting somewhere*, she thought. Part of her felt guilty for invading

Hope's privacy and reading her intimate thoughts, but based on the circumstances, she wasn't left with much choice. She looked again at the date of the entry. 1915? Yikes. They were a long way from iPods and texting.

She would have liked to learn more from the journal's pages, but there wasn't time. She returned the diary to its original place, praying that Hope would never know it had been read.

The desk had only one drawer. Maggie peered in and caught a glimpse of newspaper. She pulled the drawer open further to read the headline on the clipping. It was the same one she'd discovered just a few days ago, only now instead of being discoloured and delicate, the paper was crisp, as if it were hot off the press.

Maggie turned to the others to tell them of her discoveries, only to find Gillian sorting through the clothes in the steamer trunk. She held a simple cotton dress up in front of her. "Not really my style," she mumbled and looked back into the trunk.

"You can't wear those clothes!" Maggie said.

"Why not? Have you figured out another idea?"

"No, but those are Hope's and when she sees us she will know they're hers." Her eyes darted around the room. "Where's Cole?" She grabbed Gillian by the wrist, her own face now pale.

"He was here just a minute ago."

Suddenly, the girls heard footsteps approaching. Their eyes frantically searched the room. No escape. The single door was the only way in or out.

In a desperate attempt to hide, the girls dove under the bed. Maggie squeezed in next to Gillian beneath its tiny frame, getting an elbow in the face. Maggie's heart thumped so loudly she prayed whoever was coming wouldn't be able to hear it.

The door creaked open.

Chapter Nine

Maggie's heart hammered like a runaway train as she stole a brief look from beneath the bed. A pair of Nike sneakers walked past. Definitely not footwear from this time period.

"Hey girls, check this out!" Cole said. "Maggie? Gillian? Where are you?"

"Cole! You scared us half to death," Maggie shrieked then struggled to get out of her cramped hiding place.

Gillian popped out behind her and stretched her legs.

Maggie rushed over to her brother and wrapped her arms around him, her sudden physical affection surprising them both. She stepped back and stared down at him with a stern look. "Where were you?"

"I had to go take a look in my room. My stuff's all gone. And I've never seen it that clean before." His arms overflowed with what appeared to be clothes. "I found something though."

"You could have been caught," Maggie said. "Don't scare us like that again." She gave him a shove. Maggie had a brief vision of having to explain to her mom that she'd lost her younger brother somewhere back in time. The look on her mom's face was one of utter devastation. She ran her fingers through her hair then shook her head to clear it. "We need to stick together. Now let's see what you've got there."

Cole transferred the bundle over to his sister and she unfolded three outfits, footwear, and even a hat. Maggie thought it strange that they were all in the exact sizes and right gender for each of them. She scratched her head. "You found these in your room?"

"Yup."

"Was there a note or anything with them?"

"No. But I didn't steal them if that's what you're thinking. My room was empty and the clothes were just sitting there, folded all neat on the bed, like they were waiting for us."

Now this is really bizarre, Maggie thought. Did Hope's spirit have the power to do something like this? They needed to get changed and out of this room. Quick. Next time it wouldn't be Cole walking in on them.

Maggie updated the others on the diary entry and newspaper clipping, as she took her turn to change with some semblance of privacy. Gillian needed to show her how to attach her stockings.

"This is why I only wear dresses in the summer — when I can go barefoot or just throw on some sandals," she complained as she turned to cinch up Gillian's corset. She gave the laces an extra tug and tied them as tight as she could.

"Leave me a little breathing room, would ya?" Gillian asked.

"It's not my fault your chest is so big."

"You're just jealous."

"Am so," Maggie laughed.

Without turning around, Cole groaned. "Too much information. Can you two finish up already? I need some help with these suspenders."

Clad in their new outfits, Gillian turned to Maggie. "There's some money in the pocket of my skirt and I know I didn't put it in there!"

Gillian held it out in the palm of her hand.

Maggie examined the paper currency. It looked real to her but admittedly she wouldn't have a clue if it was counterfeit or not. She decided to think positive. *Someone is definitely looking out for us*, Maggie thought, but didn't say it. She closed her hand over Gillian's outstretched one. "Just lucky, I guess. We'll need money to pay for a room, food, and anything else we might need."

"You mean we're staying here then?" Cole asked, his eyes growing wide.

"Only until we figure out what's going on and find a way back," Maggie reassured him.

Gillian paused. "I guess we really have time warped."

Maggie nodded. "It's the only explanation."

"Either that or a padded van is coming to take us away." Gillian's eyes scanned the room, as if she expected men in white suits to arrive at any moment.

"What does she mean?" Cole inched closer to his sister.

"She's just joking. Come on."

They snatched up the clothes they'd shed and tucked them under the bed. Maggie hoped they would need them again. Sooner rather than later. She lifted the hem of her long skirt to make sure she didn't trip or stumble in the strange ankle boots. *Just think of it as wearing a Halloween costume a few weeks early*, she thought as she wobbled in her heels.

"Look out 1915, here we come," Gillian said.

Cole tipped his hat to the elderly ladies they passed in the hall then held the door to the dining room for them.

"Thank you." One woman smiled and nodded at him. "Such good manners."

"Don't thank me. Thank my mom."

"Give it a rest, Casanova," Maggie whispered.

The girls ambled with their backs stiff and straight as they wandered about the hotel. Maggie muffled a cry, shocked at the changes, as they passed through the rooms. *Deep breaths*, she thought. *Try to act normal.*

Nothing remained from the life she knew in Harmony. Maggie had made every effort since her father's death not to get attached to anyone or anything. Caring hurt too much. People could be taken away from you. Now fearing that she might never see her home or mother again, she longed for something familiar.

Maggie didn't find the hotel lavish by today's standards, and its size really classified it as more of an inn than a hotel. She guessed there to be only five guest rooms, based on the second floor layout and size of the home she knew.

The front lobby bustled with people going about their business. No one gave them a second look. Maggie never would have known it used to be their living room had it not been for the same mantelpiece around the fireplace. Their faux-finished cream walls were now covered in dark wood panelling, and heavy brocade drapes framed the windows that used to allow ample sunlight in through sheer white curtains.

A few guests sat decorously on a burgundy velvet sofa and chairs in front of a welcoming fire. The same blond-haired girl they'd previously seen now worked behind the registration desk.

"That's got to be Hope," Maggie whispered to the other two. The girl glanced up just in time to see them staring at her.

"Can I help you?" she asked.

"Um … well … we just arrived and were having a look around," Maggie said.

"What room are you staying in?"

Maggie froze. What should she say? Her mind went blank.

Gillian stepped in to the rescue. "The one with the window that looks out on the oak tree." She described the location of Cole's room.

"That's strange. I don't see a record of anyone checking into that room," the girl said.

"I'm Gillian Green, and these are my cousins, Maggie and Cole Kaufman. Nice to meet you."

"Hope Lewis. Welcome to the Morris Inn. Are you travelling alone then?"

"We came with our aunt but she's out and about somewhere."

What aunt, Maggie scoffed to herself.

"Now about your room. How long will you be staying?"

Maggie stepped in front of Gillian, determined to resume control. "We're not sure at this point."

She gestured to Gillian to hand over the money. Maggie passed half of the bills over to Hope. "Would this cover things for a while?"

"Why yes, of course. Shall I help you take your bags up to the room?"

"No thanks. We travel light," Gillian said as Maggie tugged on her arm.

"I've never seen you around town before. Where are you from?" Hope smiled at them.

Now what do we say? Maggie wondered, but Gillian wasn't fazed.

"Nowhere you've been before. Hey, cool necklace." Gillian pointed to Hope's neck.

"Cool?" Hope scratched her head and touched a hand to the base of her neck. "Thank you. I think." She shook her head and looked back at them. "Well, if there's nothing else then, I must get back to the kitchen. Dinner is served at six o'clock and is included for the guests."

"Thank you," Maggie said. Whew. That could have been close. She stared at Hope's back as she departed.

For the life of her she just couldn't fathom why Hope's spirit had brought them here. Sure, the girl had it rough, working in the hotel, missing her family, and a war going on to boot. But what could Maggie and the others do about any of that? Maybe Hope's spirit would give them a sign. Or maybe if they used the Ouija board again, they could ask it what to do.

Maggie slapped herself on the forehead. "Um, guys. We left our clothes and the board in Hope's room. We'd better hurry and switch. This might be our only chance if she is busy in the kitchen."

"Yeah. We don't need to be getting caught now," Gillian said.

Chapter Ten

"You and Cole can stand guard," Maggie said to Gillian, "and I'll sneak back up into the attic, er, I mean Hope's room, to get our stuff."

Maggie took the stairs two at a time and returned to the hallway with the board and their clothes tucked like a giant football under her arm. So far so good. Maggie just wanted to get back to the Ouija board and ask Hope's spirit what to do next. They dashed to the safety of their sleeping quarters.

"You okay?" Maggie asked Cole. He hadn't said a word since they'd met Hope and now clutched the hockey jersey he'd shed earlier to his chest.

"What about Mom? She must be going crazy wondering where we are."

"My parents probably have the police out looking for me by now. They aren't gonna let me forget about this any time soon," Gillian said.

Maggie figured it best to let Gillian's comment slide and deal with Cole. "I'm worried about Mom too," she said. More worried than she would admit. "But the sooner we figure out how to help Hope, the sooner we can get out of here." She reached out and messed Cole's hair.

It's been too long since I've done this, Maggie thought. *He's not such a bad kid. I've been so caught up with my own grief I haven't even considered what he must be going through. Or Mom, either.*

"But how do we get home?" Cole asked, as he searched his sister's face for an answer.

"How about we figure out one thing at a time?" Maggie just felt they would find a way. "Let's get back to the board," she said.

The girls moved into position, the board dormant on their knees and their fingers arranged on the pointer. Cole sat next to his sister and grabbed her by the leg.

"What are you doing?" she asked him.

"If it works again and you go home, I don't want to get left behind," he replied.

Maggie couldn't help but smile. "I'm not leaving here without you … but only because I wouldn't want to face Mom's wrath if I did."

Cole released his grip and for once didn't have a smart comeback.

Maggie shook out her hands and repositioned her fingers opposite Gillian's. "Are you here, Hope?" she asked.

She looked at Gillian, hoping for a sign that her friend felt something. Gillian shook her head. Maggie asked for Hope again.

Still nothing.

The pointer didn't budge.

"I don't get it," she said. "How can Hope ditch us now when we need her the most?"

"Beats me," Gillian said. "Maybe she can't communicate because she isn't dead yet."

"Oh my gosh, you're right!" Maggie realized at once that because they'd gone back in time, Hope's spirit didn't exist yet. But what would they do now?

"Any other ideas?" Gillian asked.

Before Maggie could formulate an answer, they heard the church bells toll and a flurry of activity outside.

"What's that?" Cole asked.

The girls shrugged. They set the board aside and hustled downstairs.

A gust of cool air smacked Maggie in the face as they stepped outside. The rain had stopped but it was as if a cloud of sadness had descended upon the village of Harmony. The townspeople all walked in the same direction, dragging their feet down the dirt street, their faces filled with what looked like fear.

"Where are they going?" Cole asked.

"I don't know. Let's follow them," Maggie said.

The kids merged in step with the group. The bells continued to ring, their gongs still loud enough to make Maggie cover her ears. She pulled Gillian close and pressed her mouth near to her so she could be heard.

"Do you think there's a funeral?"

Gillian just shrugged and continued walking. The line led them to the post office, where it stopped; a crowd already gathered. The bells faded into the distance.

Without a word, the postmaster stepped outside the front door. He slowly posted a white notice paper on the front window and with a solemn face turned back inside.

Maggie heard a gasp and then a woman at the front of the crowd wailed.

"Whatever it says, it can't be good," Gillian said.

A few at a time, people moved forward to the notice, scanned its contents, and then walked away. Their departing faces displayed one of two emotions. Grief or relief.

"Let's check it out," Maggie said.

She and Gillian moved forward with the others, Cole tucked safely between them. They were second in line now. Two men, stooped and grey haired, stood in front of them. They searched the notice.

"Looks like your boy is safe for another week," the first man said.

The second man put his arm around the first's shoulder. "I'm sorry, old chap. May he rest in peace, brave soul." The two men turned back in the direction from which they'd come, heads down, one sobbing and the other doing his best to console.

Now face to face with the announcement, Maggie understood what it was. Not a funeral — but that would only be a matter of time. Listed on a telegram were the names of soldiers who had been killed in the war in the past week. Her eyes skimmed down the list, not really expecting to see anyone she knew.

Gillian gently nudged her, pointed at a name, and said, "Edward Lewis. Hope's father is on here."

So that's why he died young, she thought. They moved aside to allow others a chance to read the list. Maggie looked back. She hadn't noticed Hope in the crowd earlier, but now she spotted her at the front. *Oh no!* Maggie thought.

Hope crumpled like a rag doll into the arms of those

next to her. Two women led her away, their arms supporting her petite frame, but unable to comfort her. Maggie's stomach churned. *I know just how she feels*, she thought. It's a terrible shock, leaving your world ripped apart. You don't even get the chance to say goodbye. And now maybe she wouldn't be able to say goodbye to her mom. Maggie swore to herself that if they ever … no, *when* they got home, she would really talk to her mother.

Hope wrenched free of the women's arms, sobbing, and stumbled blindly out onto the road. Maggie watched in horror as a team of horses came barreling through, driver and animals both oblivious to the young woman in their path.

Without a moment's thought, Maggie ran onto the road, grabbed Hope by the waist, and yanked her out of harm's way with only seconds to spare. She bent over to catch her breath, and when she raised her head she found herself looking directly into Hope's tearful eyes.

"Thank you," Hope choked out.

"Let me walk you back to the hotel," Maggie said.

Maggie stirred her stew around in her bowl at dinner that evening, but ate very little other than a few bites of bread. The animated chatter of the afternoon had been replaced only by the gentle clinks of silverware. She picked at imaginary lint on the tablecloth, her face bathed in the shadow of their table's oil lantern flame.

They hadn't seen Hope since Maggie had returned her safely to the hotel and her waiting relatives. Another teenage girl had served them their meal. The few other guests trickled out and up to their rooms, two or three at a time.

Once back in their room, Maggie settled Cole into one of the two double beds the room offered, covered him with a blanket, and then squeezed under the quilt of the other bed with Gillian.

Before long, Cole climbed onto the foot of the girls' bed.

"Can I sleep with you guys?" he asked.

"It's pretty crowded already, but I have an idea." Maggie pushed the two beds together and they all climbed back in, elbows poking and shins bumping till they'd each staked out their spots. The girls waited for the sound of Cole's snores before they spoke.

"How awful for Hope to hear about her dad that way," Gillian said in a whisper.

"Whether it's a policeman at your door or a sheet of paper on a post office wall — it knocks the breath right out of you. And there is no turning back no matter how much you want to."

"It must be terrible for both of you. Cole too."

Maggie nodded but didn't trust her voice to reply.

"You can talk to me about your dad anytime, Maggie."

"I know. Thanks."

They snuggled deeper under the quilt, trying to get comfortable amongst the bed's lumps. Maggie wasn't sure what the mattress was stuffed with but she was too tired to care. Her eyelids grew heavy. She had no idea what the next day would bring.

Maggie put her arm around Cole as he slept, curled in a fetal position. She needed him close too.

Chapter Eleven

Maggie woke to the sun's rays warming her face. *Where am I?* she wondered, but her confusion was short-lived. A glance around the room revealed that they were still in 1915 and that she was the last one up.

"I, for one, am not going to sit around crying all day," Gillian said. "I'm going to look around town." Before Maggie could protest, her friend continued. "It would be best for you guys to keep busy too until we figure things out."

"You're right," Maggie said. "But I think I'm going to look for Hope."

"Cole?" Gillian asked, indicating he could join her.

Cole looked to his sister for approval. Maggie nodded.

Maggie searched the dining room for Hope. The tables deserted and cleared of breakfast dishes, she pushed open the kitchen door.

The aroma of brewed coffee and fried bacon lingered, but the room seemed empty. Maggie was just about to turn around and leave when she heard someone sob. She took a few more steps and found Hope, scrubbing the breakfast dishes and weeping. Hope must have heard her enter, as she jumped and looked up from her work.

"I'm sorry. I didn't mean to startle you."

"It's you again. Maggie, right?" Hope wiped at her tears but instead got a face full of suds.

"Yes. Let me help you," Maggie offered, handing Hope a towel to dry her eyes.

"Thank you but you shouldn't be in here. Mr. Morris will be angry if he sees a guest in the kitchen."

Maggie ignored her warning and reached for a clean dish towel. When Hope didn't resist, the girls settled into a routine of washing and drying. The silence wasn't uncomfortable; in fact, their steady rhythm soothed Maggie. It was comforting to be next to someone who was going through the same emotions that she'd so recently dealt with. Was still dealing with, in fact. She didn't need to pretend she was okay in front of Hope.

"My dad died too," Maggie finally said.

"Too many soldiers are dying," Hope replied then sighed. "That wasn't very thoughtful of me. I don't know what I'm saying."

"It's okay. You're in shock." Maggie rubbed her arm. "Actually, it was in a car accident. Three months ago." She was grateful that Hope didn't say she was sorry. It was all people seemed to say to her lately and she didn't want pity. She didn't think Hope wanted that either.

"A car accident?" Hope asked. "You mean your family actually owns an automobile?"

"Um ... well ... it wasn't really ours." *That was sort of the truth*, Maggie thought. A drunk driver's car killed him but as Hope had probably never heard of such things, Maggie didn't offer to explain.

"Oh. Still sudden though," Hope trailed off.

Maggie nodded. "I remember the numbness and shock in the first few days. It was hard to do even the simplest things, like brushing my teeth or doing my schoolwork."

"Mr. Morris didn't make me work today. I just couldn't stand the thought of having too much time on my hands to think though, so I volunteered. Then I went and put icing sugar in the pancakes this morning instead of flour," Hope said, another tear sliding down her cheek.

Maggie smiled. She'd done similar things. "It's okay to cry. I've cried so much I should have drowned in my tears by now. If you ever want someone to talk to, I'm here." Maggie wished she could have shared her tears when they had come, but had hid them along with her pain. Perhaps Hope would find a healthier way to deal with her loss.

"And thanks to you and your quick thinking on the road yesterday. I'm still here too," Hope said and turned to embrace her. Both now covered in suds, the girls broke into a welcome giggle. Hope looked at Maggie and her grin vanished. "The memorial service is tomorrow. Mr. Morris has given me the whole day off. Do you think…?" Hope paused.

"Yes, I will go with you." The knot in Maggie's gut, the one that had been rock hard for months, started to soften. Maybe sharing your grief could actually lessen the burden.

"I quite like your hair," Hope said, seemingly eager to change the subject.

Maggie ran her fingers through her short bobbed tendrils. She hadn't thought much one way or the other about it lately. Her dad used to tell her that it was the colour of dark chocolate, matching her eyes.

"It must be so much easier to look after than these awful braids of mine. I see quite a few girls have cut theirs since the war started."

Maggie looked fondly at her new friend. It was almost as easy as talking to Gillian. In some ways, maybe easier. "I wouldn't change a thing," she assured Hope

When the dishes were dried and stacked in neat piles, the girls proceeded outside for some fresh air. Maggie figured the exercise and change of scenery would do them good.

As they walked along the streets, Hope pointed out the main buildings and their historical facts. Maggie was careful not to slip and reveal that she lived in Harmony as well, just that it was almost one hundred years later.

The familiar roads, now congested with horse and buggies, were miles apart from the usual stream of cars. An electronics outlet in Maggie's time was now the shop of the local blacksmith. The giant maples that Cole loved to climb in the park were only half their future size.

A group of people stood gathered around picnic tables and Hope led Maggie in their direction. The women must have recognized Hope since many waved at her. As they approached, Maggie heard a familiar giggle. Gillian. Leave it to her friend to find a group of gossiping women. Gillian stood in their midst, arms and head tangled in a heap of yarn.

"What in the world are you doing?" Maggie asked.

"Learning how to knit. It was going pretty well for a while." Gillian shrugged.

One of the women in the group murmured to the others, "A girl her age who doesn't know how to knit. My word. I've never heard of such a thing." The woman turned to Gillian with an exasperated grin.

A pile of socks formed in the centre of the table.

"We're sending them overseas to the men in the trenches. The weather will be turning colder soon and they'll need them," Gillian explained then lowered her voice to a whisper. "Besides, knitting is hip again back home. Think of all the cool stuff I'll be able to make."

"You'd better keep practicing then," Maggie said. "Where's Cole?" Her stomach clenched. Now more than ever, she was afraid of losing anyone else close to her.

Hope fussed with her dress and shifted nervously, obviously ready to leave. *If she's anything like me she probably doesn't feel like listening to any condolences,* Maggie thought.

"He's over there." Gillian pointed.

Cole and several other boys about the same age hit the ball and raced around bases in a last game of baseball before the crisp days of fall ended. Maggie thought they looked so cute in their bloomers and sailor-style jackets. Cole fit right in.

For a short while, the troubles of the war seemed far from their minds. Maggie waved in his direction. This is just what Cole needs today, she thought. Some normalcy, if that was possible, after you'd met a spirit and then travelled back in time.

Cole waved back, she said goodbye to Gillian and her new knitting pals, and the two girls continued on their walk.

After a few blocks, Hope spoke again. "I didn't get to say goodbye to him. Did you?"

Maggie knew immediately who Hope was referring to. She shook her head. "There are so many things I wish I'd said to my dad." She had replayed them over and over in her mind.

"If only there was some way I could talk to him again," Hope said.

A man walked down the other side of the street, hand in hand with his daughter. *She's so lucky*, Maggie thought and sighed. She glanced at Hope, whose eyes were focused on the pair as well.

"I talk to him all the time. I believe he can hear me," Maggie admitted.

She'd never shared this secret with anyone before. If it would help Hope though, it was worth it. This was the most she'd talked about her father since his death.

"I suppose you're right. But still ..." Hope left her wish hanging between them.

"Maybe there is a way. Meet me back in our room after dinner tonight?" Maggie thought that if there was a means, it would be through the Ouija board.

Chapter Twelve

Gillian looked at Maggie in shock. "You told her about the board?"

"Yeah. But only that we had one and that there was a chance we could contact her father with it. Give me a bit of credit. I didn't tell her we've already talked to her after she's dead!"

Now that Maggie had developed a friendship with Hope, she couldn't get a handle on the fact that she'd spoken with her spirit. At some point she would have to face it, but she wasn't ready yet.

"Did she freak out?" Gillian asked.

"No, not at all. She's scared but she's willing to give it a try if it means a chance to say goodbye," Maggie said.

Gillian paced in their tiny room. Cole looked at his sister, clearly doubting her judgment on this one. "But it's our secret," he said. "She might be okay with it but if she tells anyone else we're gonna be in even bigger trouble."

"Who's she gonna tell?" Maggie asked them. "She's all alone. Her family had to go back to their farm and she doesn't have any time for friends here. She needs us."

"Needs us for what?" Gillian asked. "I still don't get why we're here. Although I did meet a cute guy at the park today." This time Gillian actually blushed.

"There you go again — boy crazy even in the direst of circumstances." Maggie shook her head and continued. "I can't explain it. It just feels like the right thing to do. Maybe it will help Hope deal with her father's death."

"Okay." Gillian said. "But there's no guarantee it will work, you know."

"I know."

"Anything could happen … or nothing at all," Gillian continued.

Maggie nodded.

Cole shrugged and followed his sister's lead.

A few minutes later, there was a gentle knock on their door. Hope entered the room, her head down, as she smoothed the front of her skirt.

"You remember my brother, Cole, and my frie … um … cousin, Gillian," Maggie said. With any luck, Hope wouldn't ask where their aunt was.

"Hi," Hope said, her voice barely above a whisper.

"There's not much room, but we could all sit on the bed." Gillian scooted over and patted a spot on the quilt beside her.

Cole looked at Hope with his big, puppy-dog eyes. "I'm sorry about your dad."

"Thank you. I'm sorry about yours too," Hope said. "You look so much like my younger brother, Max. He's about your age, I suspect."

"Where is he?" Cole asked.

"He stays at home on the farm with one of my other brothers and mother. I'll be joining them tomorrow."

"Wow. You've got a big family. I only have Maggie and my mom now." Cole glanced at his sister. She knew he hadn't meant it in a bad way. She looked back at him proudly.

"And you're very lucky to have them," Hope said.

Maggie busied herself lighting the lantern on the dresser. She adjusted the wick and struggled with the wooden match sticks. Once lit, it cast a soft glow over them as they huddled together. She wanted to give her brother and friend a chance to speak with Hope a bit. She felt certain they would like her once they got to know her.

Gillian propped herself up on some pillows. "What's it like working here?"

"Not so bad really. I'm too busy to think about it much. It pays me a little bit of money that I can use to help my family with."

"It must be hard work," Gillian said. "Gee. I complain about just cleaning my bedroom."

"It is," Hope replied, "but I'm used to working hard from the farm."

"What about school?" Gillian asked.

"Oh, I've finished. I'd like to marry and start a family of my own soon."

"You're kidding me! You're too young for that." Gillian's eyes opened to an enormous size. Maggie couldn't fathom a husband or babies yet either.

"Not really. I turned seventeen last month." Hope looked to Maggie and then Gillian. "Aren't you thinking about marriage?"

"No way," Gillian said, shaking her head. "Maggie and I are only fourteen. Times sure have changed." Gillian ignored Hope's look of confusion at her last remark and continued. "And you definitely don't look your age, Hope."

"Well I feel like I've aged too much these last couple of months."

"I can relate to that," Maggie said. Sometimes she wished she had fewer responsibilities and could feel more like a kid again.

Maggie brought the Ouija box over to the bed and joined the group. She slid the lid off and withdrew the board, shivering as she touched it again.

She explained the basics about using it to Hope and then the three girls formed a triangle, much like the shape of the pointer. Maggie remained adamant that Cole not touch the board.

Hope's face began to pale. Maggie wondered if she was having second thoughts. "Are you okay?" she asked. "Do you want to continue?"

Hope nodded and gave a feeble smile.

"I'm scared too," Maggie said. "But we're all in this together and we can stop any time we want."

Maggie's instincts continued to convince her that the Ouija board held the key to solving the puzzle of their trip back in time. She shook out her arms and hands, cracked each set of knuckles, and blew out a long, slow breath. No matter how crazy or scary things got, she needed to do this for Hope. If everything went as planned they would contact Hope's father for her and no harm would come of it. Maybe this was how they would help her and then find their own way home.

She lifted her hands once more, only this time she reached out to the others. They joined hands in a circle and looked back and forth, from one to the next. Maggie smiled at each of them then returned her hands to the board, the other two girls following suit.

"Is anyone with us?" she asked.

Maggie focused on the board until her eyes were nearly blurry. She heard a collective intake of breath as they waited.

Nothing.

She tried again.

The pointer began to move, orbiting the outskirts of the wood, not remaining on any one letter. The girls held fast, until finally the pointer settled.

YES

Maggie exhaled a whoosh of breath. Unconsciously, she'd held it again. Her pulse quickened despite her attempts to calm it. She knew what she had to ask next.

"Are you Edward Lewis?" For Hope's sake, Maggie prayed it was. She looked at Hope to see how she was faring, but her new friend was so focused on the board that Maggie couldn't make eye contact.

Again the pointer took its time. There wasn't any recklessness to its movements, in comparison to their last wild ride on the board. Maggie followed its progress. The miniature wooden table looped around and finally decided to land at the bottom of the board.

NO

Chapter Thirteen

It took every ounce of Maggie's will to maintain her composure. If it wasn't Hope's father, then who was it? She'd never even considered any other possibility. What if they'd made a connection with something wicked? Was she putting her brother and friends in danger? Maggie stared at the others, unable to voice her fears.

Hope's face fell in a look of disappointment. Gillian's hands slipped from their perch and Maggie could feel Cole trembling at her side. The pointer lay at rest, unmoving.

"We have to continue," Hope said.

"What?" Maggie couldn't have heard her right. She'd failed her friend and yet she still wanted to move on. What did she know that they didn't? Did she still have an inkling of faith? Or was she merely prepared to face whatever lay ahead, regardless of the consequences?

"She's right," Gillian said. "I may not like it, but we have to find out who we've contacted."

Cole didn't speak but squeezed his sister's arm and nodded his approval. Unable to believe everyone else's reactions,

Maggie heaved a sigh. "Okay. But if it's anyone evil we're done immediately."

The girls placed their fingers back on the pointer.

"Who are you?" Maggie asked.

At first nothing happened. Just as she was about to repeat her question, there was a slight movement. Barely discernible, but there nonetheless. Slowly the words began to form.

```
It's Dad, Maggie. I'm here.
```

This time it was Maggie's fingers who fell from their perch, a moan escaping her lips.

"Put your hands back!" Cole yelled. "We can't break the connection."

Maggie froze. She wanted to believe it was her father more than anything else in the world but what if they were being tricked. What if it was a harmful spirit after all? She had to know for sure. She resumed her position.

"What's my nickname?" she asked.

Without any hesitation, the pointer slowly spelled out its message.

```
"Some Kid" and Cole's is "Pookie."
```

"It's really him!" Cole looked to his sister without the slightest hint of embarrassment over the name he'd refused to let anyone but his dad call him.

Maggie knew he was right. There was no doubt in her mind. Yet her body felt as if it were made of cement. This wasn't how she had planned it. She'd originally hoped she might connect with her father through the board, but had forgotten all about her wish after meeting Hope. She'd prayed for this moment so many times and yet now that it was actually happening, she didn't know what to do. She couldn't seem to collect herself.

```
I'm so proud of you both.
```

Tears streamed down the siblings' faces. Maggie turned to her brother. "You can talk. It's okay."

"I miss you so much, Dad," Cole said. "I love you."

The next message took a while to spell out and required all of their concentration. Cole used the notebook to record it. The second his hand stopped writing, he held up the message for everyone to read.

```
Try not to be sad. Remember the good
times. Life goes on and so must you.
I am always with you. In your hearts.
```

Maggie's heart felt like it was shattering into pieces all over again. It wasn't fair that she'd lost her dad. Why him? He'd never done anything to deserve what happened to him. She felt cheated, ripped off. He wouldn't be there when she learned to drive, went to the prom, graduated school, married, and had children of her own. Most of all, she missed him trudging into the house at the end of each day and announcing "I'm home" in his booming voice. But having this chance to speak with him again was such a gift.

The pointer spelled out the next message. Again, Cole wrote the letters down as they appeared then passed his notebook over to Maggie so she could read the message aloud. Her voice was a whisper.

```
Don't hold your grief in. Sharing it
makes you stronger.
```

Maggie began to sob. *I wish Mom was here*, she thought. She hoped some day she would be able to tell her about this special moment. Maybe it would ease her pain too.

"I love you, Dad," she said. "There are so many things I never got to tell you."

```
Talk to me anytime. I will hear you.
It's time for me to go now though.
```

"No! Please don't leave!" Maggie cried. She was desperate for more time. But deep inside she knew this couldn't last. Ending the session didn't mean letting go. She would never forget her father. She would keep him close throughout her life.

She had to ask, "Will we talk to you again?"

Back and forth, from letter to letter, the pointer spelled out its final words.

```
Not like this but in other ways. I
love you both.
```

The pointer rested on the letter H. They waited for several more minutes but no further communications came through. Gillian gently removed Maggie's hands, one finger at a time, from the pointer and started to pack the board back into its box. Hope reached over and drew the siblings into her arms.

"I'm so sorry, Hope," Maggie said and began to weep.

"Sorry? No! You don't need to apologize for anything."

Maggie saw through her tears that Hope was crying with her. Gillian joined them back on the bed, enveloping them in a group hug.

"It hurts so much," Cole sobbed.

"I know," she said.

"Do you?" he asked, breaking free and looking at her, hands on his hips. "You act like you don't care about anyone and you never want to talk about him." Cole's voice lowered again, almost to a whisper this time. "I need to talk about him or I'm afraid …"

"Afraid of what?" Maggie had to lean close to hear.

Cole stared into his lap. "I'm afraid I'll forget him."

"Oh Cole, you won't. Mom will make sure of that. And I'll try to do better too." She lifted his head up so she could see his eyes.

"Promise?" he asked.

"I promise." Maggie knew it was normal for brothers and sisters to fight but when it came right down to it she loved Cole and was sorry if she'd hurt him. She hugged him close.

Maggie had no idea how long they sat there. Her tears seemed endless.

After what felt like hours, the group untangled to prepare for bed.

"Goodnight," Hope said.

"You're welcome to stay with us," Maggie offered.

"Thank you, but I need a bit of time alone," Hope replied. "I'll see you tomorrow though."

"I understand." Maggie identified only too well. In her case though, she was ready now to let others in and escape her self-imposed solitude.

The three each gave Hope a quick hug before she left. Maggie didn't even bother to separate the beds. She made a place for Cole and motioned for him to crawl in. Snuggled close to her brother, she could still smell the fresh scent of the outdoors from earlier in the day in his hair. Gillian wrapped the quilt around them.

"I love you," Maggie said.

"Love you too," Gillian and Cole both replied.

A full moon escaped from behind the cloud cover and filled the room with light, the silence broken only by an occasional sob. The three clung together in their makeshift bed.

Maggie's last thoughts before exhaustion claimed her were that her grief felt like an earthquake. The initial blow devastated everything in its path. You grouped together, trying to recover and move on, even if it meant you'd lost the things most important to you. But when you least expected it, an aftershock would hit. It might be days, it might be months or years. Maggie knew without a doubt now, that whenever those tremors did hit she would not be alone and she would survive them.

Chapter Fourteen

"Wake up. It's time to shop!" Gillian yanked the blankets off Maggie.

"You've *got* to be joking. How can you even think about shopping?" She groaned, dove back under the covers, and stuck the pillow over her head.

Cole giggled and tickled Maggie's toes, which peeked out the end of the bed. Nothing, absolutely nothing, drove her crazier than having her feet tickled.

"Okay, okay. I'm getting up." Maggie was a mess. Her hair stuck up all over the place and she had dark circles under her eyes.

"Gillian's right. We do need a change of clothes," Cole said, sniffing under his armpits.

Maggie's antenna went on instant alert. "This coming from the kid Mom practically has to force into the shower?" she teased.

"Okay … I confess. Gillian bribed me with candy." Cole shrugged and offered a guilty grin.

"Aha! I knew it." Maggie tickled Cole under his ribcage.

"I'm going for my sponge bath. Be ready when I get back?" Gillian looked to Cole and Maggie. They wrestled playfully on the bed.

"What I wouldn't give for a Jacuzzi and a manicure right now," Gillian said with a sigh.

Maggie just smirked at her friend, seconds before Cole thwacked her over the head with a pillow.

After pancakes smothered in maple syrup in the hotel dining room, the kids strolled down the main street.

"Well I guess designer shops are out of the question," Gillian grumbled.

Maggie couldn't help but laugh, and rolled her eyes at her friend. "We can't be too long. I promised Hope I would be at the memorial service for her dad today."

Maggie felt good about her promise to attend. Last night's experience with the Ouija board filled her with a new inner strength and she was pleased she would be able to offer her support. Not that she would ever want to make attending funerals a habit. She knew that there would be many more before the war ended and even more children left without fathers.

"We'll come too, if you like, won't we Cole?" Gillian said.

"Okay. But you promised candy," He replied.

"How could you have any room left for candy after all you just ate?" Maggie asked in disbelief.

"I'm never too full for candy." Cole patted his stomach.

"Clothes first then treats." Gillian sashayed in front, in serious shopping mode.

Their lack of transportation and the time period meant a choice of exactly one store. Maggie watched with amusement as Gillian made the best of things, sorting through the racks of "vintage" dresses, giggling. Cole managed to find himself a pair of overalls and a straw hat.

"What do you think?" he asked the girls, as he modelled his new outfit.

"Cute. You're a regular little Huck Finn," Maggie said.

"Maybe I should get some rubber boots too if we're going to Hope's farm."

Hope had assured Maggie that there would be enough wagons coming for them to catch a ride and more food than they could ever possibly eat.

"Sure. Add them to the pile," she said.

Maggie chose a simple navy dress and overcoat that would also be suitable for the service. They each grabbed a couple changes of underwear, Gillian complaining about boring white cotton the entire time, and some necessary toiletries, then went to pay for their purchases.

As Maggie counted out their money, Gillian approached the store clerk and piped up, "Excuse me. Could you please tell me where your hairspray is?"

"Hairspray?" The clerk scratched his head, his face a complete blank.

Maggie elbowed her friend. Gillian looked at her as if to say "what?" Cole slapped his knee and laughed hysterically. "That's okay. This will be all," she told the clerk.

As she paid, Maggie worried about their money supply dwindling but didn't comment. No one knew at this point how long they would be here. Better not to concern the others with it.

Once outside the store, she turned to Gillian and smacked her palm against her forehead. "I can't believe you asked for hairspray! You could have given us away."

"Well do *you* know when it was invented? And my hair just won't spike right without it." Gillian pouted.

Maggie couldn't help herself — she laughed. "No I don't, but I'm sure it will be a long time yet."

"Now can we have candy?" Cole begged, his hands together in a praying gesture.

"Yes!" the girls said in unison.

The general store offered an array of choices to satisfy Cole's craving for candy. Gone were the days of one-dollar chocolate bars. Or, more correctly, those days hadn't arrived yet.

Maggie stood at the front counter. Rows of glass jars filled with sweets in every colour lined the shelves. Cole jumped up and down like a toddler when told about the concept of penny candy. He stuffed an entire paper bag full. Maggie even treated herself to a jawbreaker, her lips changing colour with each new layer exposed. Gillian opted for licorice. In a moment of weakness, Maggie decided to buy her brother a set of jacks. She thought it might be fun for him to have a game with the other boys at the farm.

"I can't wait to meet Max." Cole bounced around, already on a sugar high.

"Remember, he's just lost his father," Maggie said. "He may not be in a very playful mood." She remembered all too clearly the days following the Kaufman's own dire news.

"I know. But maybe I'll be able to cheer him up the way you have with Hope."

"You know, you're all right." Gillian smiled at him then looked to Maggie. "I guess if I had to be plunged back in time, I couldn't have picked two better people to be with."

"You're not so bad yourself." Maggie put her arm around her friend's shoulder as they walked back to the hotel.

Cole ran a few steps ahead of the girls and she turned to Gillian.

"I still feel like I haven't done enough for Hope."

"What more could you possibly do?" Gillian asked. "You're support obviously means the world to her."

They walked along a few feet before Maggie spoke again. "I can't help thinking that if we ... if we had come back in time sooner, maybe we could have prevented her father's death."

"But how? I mean you can't just go changing history!"

"Why not? Maybe we could have come before he left for the Front. Warned him not to enlist or something. I overheard some of the adults talking about conscription at the hotel. It hasn't been enforced yet so he wouldn't have had to go fight."

"What makes you thing he would have listened to you? Don't torture yourself with this. The power of the board brought us back when we were supposed to arrive. Messing with anything else has too many scary implications."

"You don't think what we've done has changed things?" Maggie asked.

"I think you've been a major help in Hope's life. You're being her friend when she needs one the most, but you haven't changed the course of bigger events."

"Okay. Maybe you're right on that. Hey ... since when did you get so smart?"

"Maybe you just never noticed before," Gillian said.

"I'm sorry." Maggie seemed to be apologizing for her behaviour a lot lately.

"No problem. Most of the time I like making you laugh and being the lighter half of our duo."

"You do have a way of making me smile," Maggie said and gave her friend a good natured shove. "But I think you're wrong about the board."

Gillian raised her eyebrows in surprise.

"I don't think the power is just in the board. I think it's in *us* too."

Chapter Fifteen

Later that morning, Hope's older brother, Adam, arrived. He hitched his team of horses to the post outside the hotel while the girls and Cole climbed aboard the wagon. Hope rode up front with her brother, while Maggie, Gillian, and Cole rested on a bed of hay in back, dangling their legs over the edge.

The farm was only about five miles from town but Maggie thought it felt further when you weren't travelling by car. If they hadn't been heading to a funeral, she might have thought it was a fun way to spend a day.

As they drove up the dirt road to the house, she noticed a crowd milling about on the front lawn. Folks had tethered their buggies and horses up all over the place, but Maggie only spotted one or two strange-looking cars. People were spreading out their blankets on the grass and sitting in front of a large willow tree.

"Why are they having the funeral at home?" Cole whispered.

Gillian shrugged. "Maybe funeral homes haven't been invented yet?"

"Probably it's because Hope's dad was killed overseas." Maggie spoke softly so that Hope and Adam wouldn't hear. "I'm guessing the family will have a private time at the cemetery once they have a stone for his grave."

They *did* know from their visit to the cemetery that eventually a tombstone was made, but Maggie wasn't sure if the bodies of soldiers were returned or not. She couldn't get the "Flanders Fields" poem out of her head, even though she'd been told that wasn't where he died.

"Well I like this better," Cole said with certainty.

They jumped down from the wagon and followed Hope toward a petite woman dressed in black, with a boy about Cole's age at her side. Her eyes were puffy and red, but she stood straight and looked directly at them. The striking resemblance left Maggie with no doubt as to whom she was.

Hope fell into her mother's arms. When she reluctantly broke her embrace, Hope introduced them, referring to Maggie and the others as her new friends and guests from the hotel.

"Any friends of my daughter are welcome in our home."

"Our deepest sympathy to you and your family," Maggie said. It was what everyone had said to her own mother and so she repeated it now.

Cole and Max gave each other a wave hello. The minister arrived soon after, which signalled the start of the service. It was a large but solemn crowd. After a number of prayers and platitudes, the minister stepped aside and let individuals share their memories of Edward Lewis. Maggie heard many speak of his bravery and charity toward his fellow neighbours. He was a well-respected and loved man.

Hope was the last to speak. Maggie looked into her eyes, offering unspoken support. She admired Hope's courage and was touched by her words of love for her father. As the tears fell down Hope's cheeks, Maggie cried along with her friend.

The service ended with a prayer, then a hundred or so voices rose in song. The words of "Amazing Grace" were known by all, even those who lived almost a hundred years in the future. Maggie sang along until she could no longer choke out the words between sobs. She hummed the last verse, her tears flowing freely down her cheeks. Gathered by the giant willow, it was as if its branches and leaves were weeping too.

As soon as the last note faded, the women in the gathering headed straight for the kitchen. The few older men in the group set up long tables on the lawn for the women to place the lunch. There were too many people to all fit in the house and though the weather was crisp, it was still suitable for an outdoor meal. The largest number in the group were definitely the children, with so many men and older boys off in the war.

"That cute guy from the park is over there. Mind if I go say hello?" Gillian asked.

"Go ahead. I'm going inside to help out, if you'll be okay Cole?"

Cole nodded and raced off to join Max and some of the younger boys who bee-lined it toward the barn and its assortment of animals.

- - -

Maggie's stomach felt like it was about to burst. With her mom working such long hours and her own culinary skills lacking, they'd been living on a lot of frozen foods lately. What a treat it had been to feast on all the delicious home-made dishes: ham, potato salad, hard boiled eggs, fresh baked bread, and apple pie with a slice of cheese to top it off.

Gillian remained glued to her new crush, whose name turned out to be Mark. Maggie whispered in her ear, "You really have a thing for guys named Mark. You sure the 'Future Mark' won't be jealous?"

"Someone really should be leaving now," Gillian huffed, but Maggie knew she wasn't really angry.

Maggie excused herself and wandered off. Cole and Max and a group of boys were caught up in the game of jacks, so she felt safe going for a walk in search of Hope. She found her alone, leaned up against the willow tree's trunk.

She gathered the fabric of her dress tight and carefully sat on the blanket beside her. The canopy of the willow's branches and leaves formed a safe haven to view the activities of the others. Maggie felt comfortable just being together, watching fluffy white clouds drift through a sky the bluest she'd ever seen. The sun would soon be setting and the temperature would plummet.

Eventually, Hope turned to her with swollen eyes. "I haven't told you about Franz yet."

Maggie nodded, encouraging Hope to continue.

"I really love him. He's the one I plan on marrying but …"

"What is it?" she asked, leaning forward.

"He wasn't here today and I haven't heard from him."

"I'm sure he must have had a very good reason," Maggie said.

Hope pulled a wadded up handkerchief out of the sleeve of her dress and dabbed her eyes. "I suppose you'll be leaving soon."

"No. I'd planned to ride back to the hotel with you tonight."

"Actually I think I will stay here with Mama and go back in the morning. Adam will still drive you back … but that's not what I meant."

"Oh?"

"I mean you'll be leaving Harmony soon. Going home."

How could Maggie possibly answer this? If she was truly a tourist or guest just passing through town, how would she explain an extended stay? She didn't know if they would ever leave or if they could be zapped back to the future at any second.

"I'm not sure when we're leaving." Maggie hoped this answer would suffice. "But what do you say we just not worry about it right now?"

"Sounds good to me." Hope managed a small smile. "Thank you for being here today."

"I'm glad if it helped you." Maggie said.

It helped me just as much, she thought.

Chapter Sixteen

True to her word, Hope returned to work the next day. Maggie felt sorry for her that she didn't have the luxury of taking time off. With the war escalating, she guessed there were fewer people left to fill all the jobs.

Maggie figured keeping busy would be the best thing though for Hope right now. She knew it had helped her. Maggie lent a hand with the breakfast cleanup and tidied the guest rooms alongside her. Mr. Morris, the hotel owner, didn't notice a thing and Hope had been glad for both the company and assistance.

Later that afternoon, Hope headed upstairs for a short nap before she was needed in the kitchen again. Maggie sat curled up in a fireside armchair leafing through a copy of *Black Beauty*, one of the few titles she recognized. She wasn't exactly reading yet but it was a step in the right direction.

Suddenly, Adam burst into the hotel lobby and rushed over to her.

"Have you seen my sister?" He struggled to catch his breath.

"What's wrong?" Maggie asked. *Please don't let it be anything else bad*, she thought.

"I need to talk to her right away!"

She leapt from her chair and led Adam upstairs to the attic room. Adam banged on the door with his fist. Hope's face was creased with pillow case lines, and she stood rubbing her eyes as she opened the door.

"What are you doing here, Adam? Shouldn't you be at home?"

Adam pushed past her into the room and paced back and forth. His stocky build so large a presence, it engulfed the tiny bedroom. Maggie stood in the doorway listening.

"I finished the errands in town after dropping you off this morning. Halfway home, some fellas stopped my wagon and told me the news."

"What news?" Hope leaned closer toward her brother. Maggie found herself inching into the room. Adam's huge hands clenched and unclenched at his sides. He towered over his sister but when he looked down at her, his face was filled with tenderness.

"Hope, I'm so sorry. It's Franz …"

Maggie rushed up beside her just as her friend's legs began to wobble. Hope simply stared at her brother's face, her eyes completely blank.

"His whole family is gone." Adam reached out and took one of Hope's petite hands in his. To Maggie, it seemed to disappear.

"Gone? Gone where?" Hope asked, still obviously baffled.

"I don't know," Adam said. "But talk has it that their house has been completely ransacked and there's no trace of them. It's possible they were captured and sent to an internment camp."

Captured? Internment camp? Being an avid reader, Maggie recalled some internment camps of the Second World War, but had no idea that these horrid camps were also a part of the First. She'd guessed Franz was German — the name gave it away. But she was sure Hope wouldn't be friends with anyone who'd done something wrong. Then again, from what she understood, you didn't even have to do anything wrong to be imprisoned.

"Oh God." Hope moaned and started to sway as if she were about to faint. Maggie reached out to steady her and Hope continued.

"The government encouraged them to come to this country for a better life and this is what they get? They don't deserve this — they're good people."

"We know that, but obviously some people don't. Or don't care, for that matter." Adam started to pace again. "I hate this prejudice!" He punched the palm of his other hand. "If I could get my hands on the people who did this …" His voice trailed off.

Maggie couldn't stay silent a moment longer. "Please don't worry Hope. I'm sure everything will be fine."

"Fine? How can everything be fine when Franz will be forced to work like a slave, not be fed or clothed properly, and we'll be apart for who knows how long, maybe forever." Hope choked out the last words.

"I'm sorry, I didn't realize," Maggie said.

"What will I do?" Both brother and friend moved closer to Hope, the first rubbing her back and the second holding her hand as she continued. "I just knew something was wrong when I hadn't seen or heard from him this past week. How will I ever find him when I don't know which camp? I don't understand why the government has even made these internment places. It's not fair!" Tears slid down Hope's cheeks.

"Nothing about this war is fair," Adam said.

Adam promised to send news if he heard anything further but had to get back to the farm. Maggie stayed by Hope's side for the rest of the day. She wanted Hope to ask Mr. Morris for more time off, considering this latest development, but Hope wouldn't hear of it. She thrust herself back into work and helped the cook prepare supper for the guests.

Maggie met up with Cole and Gillian at the dinner table. "So what were you guys up to today?"

"Gillian took me to the park. She was all goo-goo eyed over that guy again." Cole stuck his finger partway in his mouth to emphasize his disgust.

"His name is Mark, twerp." Gillian's brow furrowed. "And we were just talking."

That's odd, Maggie thought. *Gillian never takes anything too seriously. I wonder what's up?* She wasn't about to encourage their battle though, so she recounted the news of Franz's disappearance instead.

"Poor Hope," Gillian said. "She must be freaking out."

Cole ate like he'd never seen food before, but added between mouthfuls, "It's like something out of the movies. Here one minute then gone the next."

"Do you think we're supposed to help with this? I mean do you think this is what Hope's spirit meant when she said she needed help?" Maggie looked to her friend and brother for feedback.

"What … like start our own search party or something?" Gillian's perfectly plucked eyebrows rose.

"Is does sound pretty dangerous." Cole stared at Maggie, his fork midway to his mouth.

"I suppose you're both right. Nothing we can do."

Maggie looked down at her half-eaten dumplings, silently refusing to give up. After talking further with Adam she'd learned that the camps were too far away for the kids to get there without transportation.

That eliminated a rescue mission; unless they were prepared to hop on one of the trains going north or west to the camps and risk the chance of being imprisoned themselves. But there had to be something they could do.

She pushed her plate away. She wasn't sure what to think. Would she ever really know the reason they'd come back in time? What *exactly* was their purpose here? She wished she knew the answers.

Chapter Seventeen

Gillian brushed her teeth with a smidgen of baking soda they'd picked up at the general store. Cole flopped on the bed.

"Man, I miss TV!" he said. "And fast food, and the internet, and my video games ..."

"And hairdryers, and nail polish, and shopping, and cell phones!" Gillian chimed in.

Maggie had made them all check their pockets for their cell phones when they'd realized they were stuck back in time. They'd come up empty handed with nothing of their former lives transported with them. It wasn't like they could call through time anyway, she now realized, let alone the charges for such a call even if it did exist. She laughed at the others and excused herself to go check on Hope. The halls deserted at this late hour, she tiptoed down the corridor in her nightgown. Her bare feet tread soundlessly on the wood floors.

As she climbed the attic stairs for the second time that day, she relived the events of the past few days. Had it only been a few days? It seemed like ages since she'd been home, yet in reality she *was* home, just in a different part of the time continuum.

Maggie still found it hard to grasp. These were the same stairs she would scale when she returned to the future. The same rooms she would call home. The same walls and roof that would surround and protect her. Different, yet the same. That thought alone comforted her. She knew she would make it home somehow. She couldn't stop believing in that.

She stared at the wooden railing guiding her hand. Her gut instinct told her that soon they would return to their lives in the future. *This time I'm not just going to go through the motions*, she thought. *I'm tired of missing out on the good stuff these last few months.* But oh how she'd miss Hope.

A sliver of lamplight snuck out from beneath Hope's door into the hallway, guiding her steps. Maggie knocked softly.

"Come in," Hope said.

Maggie's eyes met a vision of Hope she'd not witnessed before. Her friend sat by the window, brushing out her pale blond hair, no longer constricted by braids or a bun but falling in smooth waves down her back.

With each stroke, the soft flame of the lamp created nearly an ethereal effect. Maggie shook the image from her mind. *She's so beautiful and she doesn't even realize it. More so when she is sad.* She would never forget how Hope looked at that moment.

"Hey," Maggie said. "You okay?"

"I'm holding up."

"You're stronger than you even know." Maggie sat on the edge of the bed.

"I don't know about that." Hope continued brushing.

Maggie looked directly into her eyes, deep blue pools of sorrow. "I have a feeling things will work out fine."

"You keep saying that, but how do you know?" Hope laid her brush on the desk and moved to join her.

Maggie's fingers traced the intricate pattern of the threads in the quilt. She wondered if Hope and her mother had sewn it together. "I can't explain it."

She couldn't tell Hope that she'd seen her gravestone and that it described her as a mother and wife with a long life ahead of her. Maggie didn't even know if Franz was the one Hope was meant to share her life with. She just had a strong hunch.

"Trust me," was all she said. "This sadness will pass."

Funny, those were the exact same well-meaning words she'd been hearing for the last three months and had ignored.

"I'm going to miss you," Hope said.

"I'll miss you too." Maggie reached inside the collar of her nightgown and withdrew her most prized possession; a heart-shaped locket on a filigree gold chain. Her father had given it to her for Christmas the previous year.

Without hesitation, she unhooked the delicate clasp, removed it from her own neck, and placed it around Hope's.

Hope's eyes filled with tears. "I can't accept this," she said.

"Yes you can. And whenever you see it think of me."

"Then I will wear it close to my heart."

In turn, Hope grasped a simple wooden cross on a leather choker, hidden beneath her nightclothes, careful not to tangle it with the gift she'd just received.

"My father gave me this for my sixteenth birthday." She placed it around Maggie's neck. "I want you to have it."

Maggie began to sob. It was the most extraordinary gift she'd ever received, next to her father's. The girls embraced in a lingering hug.

When they finally pulled apart Maggie swiped the tears from her eyes. "Would you look at me, bawling all over the place? I'm going to flood your room." This brought a smile to Hope's face. "Are you sure you wouldn't rather have a sillier, happier friend?"

"I'm absolutely sure. What I needed most was someone who understood me. You've done that for me, Maggie. I can't thank you enough."

"You already have," Maggie said. She'd found just the friend she needed at this point in her life too. It was amazing how close she felt to Hope in such a short time. "Now about this Franz guy …"

"Yes?" Hope's body visibly tensed. She need not have worried.

"Is he cute?"

"He's very handsome." Hope's fair skin blushed and her shoulders relaxed.

"More importantly, is he kind?"

"Oh yes … and patient and loving and very funny." Hope beamed as she spoke of him.

"It's good to have a guy who can make you laugh," Maggie said. "So Gillian tells me, at least. Will you do me a favour though?"

"Anything," Hope replied.

"When Franz gets back — and I'm sure he will, because sooner or later either the government will realize how wrong they are or this awful war will end — hang on to him tight and love him with all your heart."

"Maybe I'll even name my first baby after you." Hope smiled.

"Unless it's a boy!"

Both girls giggled, their tears subsided.

"The second one then," Hope assured her. "Franz loves children."

Maggie squeezed her friend again then got up and stalled at the door. She didn't want this moment to end, but knew Hope needed some rest. She turned back to Hope one last time before leaving.

"Sleep well," she said.

As she descended the attic stairs to rejoin the others, her hand moved to her throat and the gift she'd received. She lovingly stroked her fingers back and forth over the smooth wood of the cross.

Chapter Eighteen

Cole scrunched his nose up and scratched his head, messing his morning bed head even further. "Maggie?"

"Yeeesss," She stretched her arms and legs like a cat. Still in the big bed, blankets tangled, she'd been lost in her own thoughts. Gillian lay beside her, and Maggie suspected she was daydreaming about a certain boy. Another day in the past had arrived and so far no further tragedies, but it was early yet.

"I was just thinking," Cole continued. "How come we could talk to Dad through the board and not Hope's spirit?"

"He's right." Gillian sat up. Apparently she wasn't that far off in dreamland. "Remember how she wouldn't answer and we thought it was because she isn't dead yet?"

This journey had taught Maggie not to dismiss anything her friend said anymore. Behind the silliness, she had discovered a serious and thoughtful girl. She didn't come out often but when she did, Maggie was ready to listen now. She nodded.

Maggie wouldn't soon forget who they'd spoken to through the Ouija. Then all her jumbled thoughts cleared at once, like finding the neon red exit sign after being lost in a museum.

"That's it!" A smile of complete joy spread across her face. "Dad's not dead yet either. He isn't even born yet!"

"And that makes you happy because...?" Gillian trailed off.

"Because it means ... it means it doesn't matter whether they're dead yet or not ... in whatever time?" Cole guessed.

"Exactly!" Maggie grinned. "I think we can use the board again to reach Hope. The power is within *us*. Why would spirits care about time? Why not just go where they need or want to?" The thought of timelessness eased the pain in her heart a bit further. Maggie stopped herself for a second though. She better get to the point before she lost them. "I think *we* were the ones who weren't ready to go home before."

Maggie grabbed Cole around the waist and squeezed him in a bear hug so tight he squealed. "Hey! What's that for?"

"Little brother, you've just helped us figure out how we're going to get home. If Hope can send us here, I'm betting she can take us back too."

Cole pumped his fist in the air as if he'd just scored a touchdown and began to jump up and down on the bed. "See! I told you it was a good idea to bring me along."

Maggie laughed. She felt giddy and joined her brother in jumping. Gillian just sat there, her body rising and falling with each bounce.

"I hate to break up the party," she said. "But what if you're wrong and Hope's spirit isn't ready to send us back home?"

The siblings stopped simultaneously. Cole tumbled off the bed from the sudden halt.

"Well I don't know for sure. But if we're not meant to find Franz, then what else could we possibly do?" Gillian didn't answer her right away so Maggie continued. "And you were the one who told me we've done all we can. Why the sudden change of heart?"

Gillian said nothing. She just stared into her lap.

"I bet it's because of Mark," Cole said, but this time without any teasing in his tone.

"Gillian?" She looked to her friend in surprise. "Don't you want to go home?"

"Well, yeah … sure." But Gillian didn't look sure to Maggie. "I really like him is all."

"Oh crud." Maggie felt awful now. She never dreamed of causing her friend any pain by this quest to help Hope. And she knew Hope hadn't meant to hurt them either.

"I'm going to miss Max too." Cole's earlier giddiness was gone.

"Listen, you guys," she said. "I know how you feel. I can't imagine not being friends with Hope after all we've been through — but we have to go home!"

Maggie rose from the bed and marched to the window. She gazed down at the street below. Her street. The one she walked every day, whether it was in this time period or the one she called home. She'd sunk them into this mess, and she was going to dig them out of it.

She turned around. "I have an idea." She forged ahead. "Gillian, you spend the day with Mark. Cole, you spend it with Max. I'll find a ride for you to the farm and back."

Maggie paced in front of the others, thinking out loud. "I'll hang out with Hope. We all make the best of every minute we have left and then tonight … tonight we get the board out and go home."

She stared at them, waiting for an affirmative response.

"Okay. I'm in." Cole placed his hand out at waist height, face down. Maggie placed hers on top of it and looked at her friend.

"Me too." Gillian placed her hand on top of the others. "If I have to go another day without shaving my legs, I'll go mad."

The day sped by. Maggie enjoyed her time with Hope and did her best not to worry that her behaviour might seem off. She didn't want Hope to suspect anything as she couldn't bear a formal goodbye. In her heart she knew it was wrong not to tell Hope they'd be leaving, but she just couldn't figure out a way to explain.

They went for another long walk, through town and to the gardens at the edge of the park. Maggie wandered over to a rose bush, the soft and fragrant scent drawing her in. She found a flush of the palest pink blooms.

Hope walked up beside her. "Beautiful, aren't they?"

She nodded. Call her a romantic, but roses were her favourite flower. Hope reached out to pluck one from the bush.

"Ouch!" A pinprick of blood appeared on her finger.

"Are you okay?" Maggie asked.

"It was worth it." Hope smiled. "I can't stop going into the garden just because it might hurt. I know this will die eventually but I want to enjoy it for as long as I can."

Both girls smiled. Maggie stepped along the worn stone path which led them back to the street. She would remember the roses fondly.

Maggie knew her strategy for getting home had the potential to fail. She focused all her energy on positive thoughts. If the power was truly within *them*, then she had to believe it with all her heart.

Chapter Nineteen

Cole dove into his evening meal like he hadn't eaten in weeks. *The fresh air and play time have definitely worked up his appetite*, Maggie thought, as she watched him reach for his second helping and then smother everything on his plate in gravy.

"I could get used to all this home cooking," she said. "You guys don't have to make suppers at home so you can't appreciate all the work that went into this."

"I'll help more when we get back if it means I get to eat more." Cole guffawed then bit into his third drumstick of chicken.

Gillian laughed at his antics. Seconds later Maggie shuddered like a skittish colt when Hope rushed up to their table.

"I've got news!"

Maggie's heart hit the floor. *Not more bad news*, she prayed.

Hope held up an envelope, her grin easing Maggie's overworked nerves. "I got a letter from my brother, Luke, who's over fighting on the front. He's okay!" Hope opened it up and set the letter down on the table for the others to read.

Dearest Hope,

I'm sorry this letter has taken so long to write. Know that as I write this that I am safe. Whenever I am not fighting, I am busy working to build trenches. The hardest part is keeping dry. I've never seen so much rain and mud. Please thank the women for all of the socks. Our feet sure appreciate them so keep them coming. I can't believe how long it's been since I have seen all of you.

Time has become a blur. I've come to realize that there is no glamour in warfare. I've seen things that I cannot even speak to you of. But I will stand tall and I will survive. I shall not let Father's death, and those of many other men, be for nothing. Please know that he fought bravely, without hesitation, and that he did not suffer. I believe he is watching out for me now ... and for all of you too. Stay strong and do not worry. I am wet and tired, but I am well.

Your Loving Brother,
Luke

"That's great news," Maggie said. "I just know things are going to be okay from here on in."

"I'm feeling much better now that I've heard from him," Hope said. "He's one less person to worry about, at least for the time being."

"I'm sure the rest of your family will be relieved too." Maggie felt less guilty about leaving, seeing that Hope's spirits were lifted somewhat.

"I knew it was a good idea for me to help the ladies with their knitting," Gillian chimed in.

Everyone laughed. Maggie didn't have the heart to tell her friend that her socks, tangles and all, probably never left town.

"I'd better get back to the kitchen. If Cole keeps eating like that I'll have to make more food." Hope smiled then turned to leave.

Cole grabbed a napkin and tried to tidy his messy hands. He completely missed the glob of mashed potatoes stuck to his cheek.

"Keep us posted?" Maggie asked.

"Absolutely." With that, Hope returned to the kitchen.

"Well that's good news," Gillian said. "We needed a bit of that."

Maggie leaned back in her chair, her belly full to bursting, and stared at Cole in wonder as he polished off a massive piece of chocolate cake. Just as she was about to comment on his insatiable appetite or the need to ration during a war, an older couple rose from the next table, deep in conversation.

As they passed by, she couldn't help but overhear the man's words.

"… and the train is leaving tonight." He glanced down at his watch. "Within the next hour, I'm told. It will be full of the folks they're taking to the internment camps."

His female companion shook her head and sighed as they left the room.

"Did you hear that?" Maggie asked. She shoved her chair back and stood up so suddenly their glasses rattled and nearly spilled. They were the only ones left in the dining room now.

"Uh huh," Gillian said but didn't move. Cole just nodded and steadied the table.

"Now what do we do?" Maggie asked. She couldn't believe it. They were supposed to be going home tonight! Yet she couldn't turn her back on what she'd just heard.

"Do you really think Franz is on that train?" Gillian asked.

Maggie nodded. She felt it in her gut. Could there be any other explanation for them overhearing that conversation? "We've got to stop that train!"

"Oh no." Gillian groaned. "It's too far and there is no way I can run fast enough after pigging out like that."

"Yeah, Maggie," Cole said.

Gillian rubbed her stomach and added, "Hope should go. She needs to see Franz, not us."

They're probably right, Maggie thought, but she'd seen Mr. Morris in the hotel earlier and there might not be time to sneak Hope out. Asking him straight out for Hope to go would be pointless too, as knowing the danger involved, he'd never let Hope leave.

Maggie stomped around the table trying to clear her head. They needed a plan. "Think, think, think," she muttered.

"Maybe we could disguise her," Gillian suggested.

Maggie shook her head. "It won't work. Not enough time.… I've got it!" she said. It wasn't the best idea and far from foolproof, but the clock ticked on. She prayed everything would turn out alright and that they'd make it through safely. Maggie wasn't normally very religious but silently crossed herself anyway and filled the other two in, laying out everyone's roles.

God help us, she thought. If anything went wrong, not only would they be stuck in the past, but stuck in prison too.

Chapter Twenty

Maggie peeked out the dining room door into the lobby and spied Mr. Morris at the front desk. She'd made the right decision — no way would Hope have made it past him.

The girls had drawn sticks, since they couldn't find any straws. Maggie ended up with the short one so she would be going with Cole, who had the only riding experience in the group. Gillian would sneak in the back kitchen entrance to tell Hope the news. "Glad I'm outta the action, er … um … I mean good luck," Gillian said and gave them a thumbs up.

Maggie and Cole rushed through the lobby and out the front door. Mr. Morris looked their way but didn't pay much attention to them. He was too busy waving his hands about as he spoke to the couple they'd seen in the dining room.

Once outside, Maggie whispered to her brother. "I can't believe we're about to steal a horse."

"It's not stealing though, right, cause we're gonna give it back as soon as we're done with it," Cole said.

Several horses stood tied up. Maggie looked them over and then chose a chestnut-coloured quarter horse with a white blaze down the front of his face. He seemed the friend-liest to her, not to mention much smaller than the others. He nuzzled at her as she stood beside him. As she reached out to stroke his mane, he gave a soft whinny in reply.

"Good horsey," she said and poked her head underneath his belly to make sure he really was a *he*. "Good boy."

She continued to pat him, trying more to control the butterflies in her own stomach than actually calm the horse down. "You said you rode when you were out at the farm?" she asked her brother.

Cole nodded. "And at camp the last two summers." He looked thrilled about this part of their adventure, unless the ants in his pants were from fear rather than excitement. Maggie dreaded it, but she'd lost the draw fair and square.

"You get on first." She cupped her hands to give her brother a boost up. Cole mounted and sat tall and proud on the horse's back, waiting. His eyes scanned the darkness, keeping watch until his sister joined him.

Maggie had never been on a horse in her life. She wasn't what you'd call a city kid, but her life in Harmony was a far cry from this. She admired the beauty and power of horses but didn't have a clue how to ride one. *Maybe this isn't such a good idea after all*, she thought. *I won't be much help if I kill myself.*

A wooden block sat by the hitching post. She assumed it was there to help riders mount.

"Hurry up before someone sees us!" Cole reached a hand out to her. "You can do it."

Maggie pulled the block over to the horse, stepped on, and then swung her leg up and over, nearly falling off the other side. She righted herself and, once seated behind her brother, looked down at the ground. "Oh boy," she said, "it looks so much higher from up here."

Her arms and legs shook. *It's now or never*, she thought. If luck was on their side, the horse's owner wouldn't even notice he was gone.

Cole grabbed the reins, clicked his tongue and they were off. Maggie almost fell at the sudden jolt and quickly grabbed her brother around the waist. They trotted down the main street, unsure exactly which way to go.

Maggie spotted a couple out for a leisurely walk on the opposite side. "Can you tell us the way to the train station, please?" She called out to them.

"Certainly. A couple of miles that way, just outside of town." They pointed in the direction the kids were already going. "Are you children alright?"

"Oh … um … yes. We're fine." Maggie hadn't even thought about them being out alone at night. Back home no one would have looked twice. Unless they recognized that the horse wasn't theirs. "Thank you," she said and waved. "Let's get out of here. Quick," she whispered to Cole.

"Hang on." Cole nudged the horse's sides and they picked up speed. Maggie had to force her mouth shut to choke down a scream.

"Breathe, Maggie," Cole said. "Horses can sense fear." He urged the horse on faster and faster. It was all Maggie could do to keep from falling. Cole's feet hung in the stirrups, leaving hers dangling without support. She did her best to wrap her lanky legs around the horse's middle and clung tighter to her brother.

They galloped full out, nervous sweat pouring down Maggie's forehead. Her heart beat as fast as the horse's hooves flew over the dirt road. She had to admit that it was less bumpy now that they'd picked up momentum, almost a rocking motion, although terrifying to her all the same.

She wasn't afraid of much, so her fear of horses didn't really make any sense — it just was. *Please let us make it in time*, she prayed. *And let me survive this ride without any broken bones, if it's not too much to ask.*

Maggie heard the sound of the train whistle up ahead and Cole shouted over his shoulder. "We're not going to make it! I can't make him go any faster!"

The road turned, curving round to the station. Maggie could just make out the back of the train, a dark red wooden car, with slats in between the planks. It looked like something they would use to haul animals, not people.

Almost there. Just another minute or two. She felt herself instinctively lean forward into Cole, both of them urging the horse on. As the station came into full view, Maggie noticed, with relief, a few men still left on the platform, boarding the train. The last man in line seemed to hesitate. It was almost as if he were waiting for someone.

If anyone noticed the two kids racing frantically down the road on horseback, they gave no indication. Several official-looking men, possibly soldiers, although Maggie wasn't certain, carried on about their business, loading the last of the cargo and people on board. Steam poured from the train, ready to leave at any second.

A small group stood huddled on the ground, sobbing and blowing kisses up to the faces peering out. Maggie wondered why they weren't being forced to go too. Could it truly all come down to what your last name was? How did they really pick and choose who went and who stayed behind?

And why wasn't anyone resisting? She knew they would have had to take her kicking and screaming. Then again, it was easier to think that when you weren't the one actually being taken away.

The pounding of the horse's hooves thundered in Maggie's ears. The wind whipped past them as they rode on. For a fleeting moment, she questioned how they would ever stop the animal beneath them. She feared they would plow on through, right into the train. At the speed they were going, one wrong move would leave a mess of broken bones on the ground. Maggie had never been so scared in her life.

Her attention quickly returned to the scene in front of her. She peered around Cole's body once more, careful not to lose her balance. Her eyes watered from the wind rushing by, but Maggie could still make things out.

The last man had boarded. The train's whistle blew again and the procession of cars slowly began to pull out.

Chapter Twenty-One

"Stop!" Maggie screamed. "Stop!"

Her cries were drowned out by the wind and the engine's wheels clacking down the track. Cole tugged on the reins, a give and go motion, to gradually slow the horse down. They slid to a halt at the edge of the tracks, a cloud of dust rising around them. They were too late.

When the dirt settled, Maggie stared in silence as the locomotive dwindled smaller and smaller in the distance, her eyes unblinking, until the darkness finally swallowed the tiny black speck.

She turned around, hoping for answers, only to find the platform deserted. She wanted to pound her fists and shout at the world in frustration. The group of supporters staggered back down the road toward town. All that remained were a few crinkling fall leaves, blowing eerily in circles from an unseen blast of air.

Maggie jumped down from the horse, her legs buckling beneath her. She was shaky and heartbroken. She stumbled over to a wooden bench under a small shelter and collapsed. She bent forward, her face in her hands, and wept. A tender hand brushed her shoulder and Maggie looked up.

"Please don't cry," Cole said. He'd dismounted and had led their steed up beside her. As if the horse felt her pain too, he gave a loud nicker and sputtered. Maggie held out her hand and the horse nudged her then slobbered in her palm.

"I blew it."

"No. We did the best we could." Cole continued to rub his sister's shoulder. "No one else would have made it either."

"How can I go back to the hotel and face Hope now?"

"Come on. We'll do it together," Cole said. He placed his arm underneath Maggie's and helped her to her feet.

"Thanks for staying calm and cool," she said. "You were awesome with that horse." She gave Cole a leg up but shook her head when he reached his arm down to her. "I think I'll stay down here on the ground."

The walk would help clear her head and she'd had quite enough riding for one night. A full moon snuck out from behind the clouds and lit their way back to town.

Grateful to be able to tie the horse back up exactly where they found him, no worse for wear and undetected, Maggie walked back to the hotel entrance with Cole at her side. She ached from head to toe, in places she never even knew existed before. She dragged her feet, simply from fatigue, as she knew full well she couldn't postpone the news to Hope any longer.

No sooner had they reached the front door when Maggie heard shouting.

"I demand to see the Kaufmans. Where are they?" a man's voice boomed.

That's us, Maggie thought. *Oh no! They found out we took the horse after all.*

"They're Germans and should have been on that train tonight."

Or not, Maggie shuddered. This was far worse than equine theft.

"I have no booking in my hotel register for anyone of that name," Mr. Morris replied.

"We will search every inch of this hotel till we find them then," the man's voice thundered again.

Oh no, Maggie thought. Before she could grab Cole and run, a hand covered her mouth, and her body was yanked from behind.

Maggie kicked with all her might and swung her elbows. *They're not taking me without a fight*, she thought.

"Uhhh!"

She spun around to find Gillian holding her stomach. Hope stood holding Cole by the arm.

"What are you two doing here?" Maggie asked.

"Trying to save you," Gillian groaned, still doubled over in agony.

"Hurry! This way," Hope said, leading them through a dark alley behind the hotel.

"Wait," Maggie said. "We haven't done anything wrong."

"Neither did Franz," Hope replied.

Maggie knew she was right, as unfair as it was. Hope stopped at a small door Maggie had never noticed before. She realized that back home it was hidden because of the lilac bushes that had been planted there.

"This will take you directly up to my attic room," Hope said. "Go quickly and hide. I'll distract the officers. Maybe they won't look there."

Maggie reached out and grasped her arm. "I'm so sorry. We didn't make it in time to stop the train." There … she'd said it.

"You risked your life for me. And you too, Cole. How could I ask any more from you than that?"

Tears sprang to Maggie's eyes once again. She was physically and emotionally exhausted. Now Hope was putting herself in jeopardy for them. Surely she would be punished somehow if the officers discovered she was covering for them.

Hope continued. "The fact that you even tried means the world to me. Now I shall help you."

Gillian moved closer. "She's right, Maggie. And Hope … even if they didn't succeed, you have to keep the faith. Franz will be fine and someday soon he'll return to you."

"Now hurry!" Hope said and gave them a quick wave before she turned and ran back down the alley.

This had to be the longest day of Maggie's life. Upon closing the outer door, the group was plunged into darkness. When her eyes adjusted, all she could make out was a faint light at the top of the stairwell, peeking out from under the door to Hope's attic room. She stumbled up the stairs with the others, hands on the rough walls, guiding her way. Even in the darkness, Maggie could feel the spider webs intruding on their path. Cole did his best to swat them away as he took up the lead. Neither of the girls complained.

Without the benefit of ventilation the air was thick. Maggie had to gulp in a breath as they rose, step by careful step. Gillian faltered on a loose board but quickly regained her footing.

At last they reached the entrance leading into Hope's quarters. Cole tried the handle without success, then gave the door a shove. He turned to the others. "It's stuck," he said, jiggling the doorknob again.

"No," Maggie said. "It has to open!"

"We're trapped!" Gillian cried.

Cole slammed into the door with his shoulder, like a hockey player making a hard check. Still nothing.

Could Hope have forgotten it was locked in some way or not realized it was blocked? Maggie wondered. *She wouldn't have sent us this way otherwise.* Maggie reached past Cole and grabbed the door handle herself. She yanked and pulled and pushed back and forth.

Still nothing, and time was running out.

Chapter Twenty-Two

The sound of boots circling the building could be heard through the thin walls of the stairwell.

"I guess we can't go back down," Maggie sighed. It would mean turning themselves in, and that was not an option. She'd stopped shoving on the door, afraid the men outside would hear, and now the three stood silent in the darkness, huddled on the top three stairs.

"Wait," Gillian said. She manoeuvered past the siblings and began to feel around the door frame. Finally, she pointed to a small hook lock, just above their eye level. Maggie would never have noticed it in the dim light but realized now that they had the same kind of outdated security in the bathroom back home. Gillian popped the small metal clasp from its hole and the door opened easily.

No sign of any officers yet. They had to get out of there. Every second counted. It would only be a matter of time before they started searching the rooms.

Until then it hadn't even dawned on Maggie that they'd been at risk. Somewhere in the back of her mind, she'd connected her last name with being German, but that was it. No one in her family spoke the language, and as far as she knew, her relatives had been in the country for generations. *This is so infuriating*, she thought. *I've never had someone be prejudiced against me because of my name. Or any reason, for that matter.*

"What about our stuff?" Cole asked. "We can't let them find it."

Gillian raised her head from between her knees, ending her calming breaths. "I'll go," she said. "The two of you can't be seen."

Gillian was right, but it didn't mean Maggie had to like yet another friend, her best friend at that, putting herself at risk for them.

"Please be careful," Maggie said and pulled Cole close.

Maggie poked her head out the attic door. The stampeding of boots and the shouts of officers echoed up from the floors below. *Oh please hurry, Gillian*, she thought.

Maggie felt like they were being hunted down by a pack of dogs. She could picture them, ripping rooms apart downstairs, like a robbery gone awry. *I'm so sorry for all the trouble we've caused*, she silently apologized. She could only imagine what Hope, Mr. Morris, and the other guests were going through down there.

It was time to go home.

Gillian charged into the room, the board tucked under one arm and their clothes spilling out of her grasp. "Time to get changed," she said.

Maggie wouldn't have slowed down for a wardrobe adjustment had it not been for fear of them leaving their modern clothes and evidence behind, and Hope to deal with an explanation she couldn't have understood.

Cole turned his back while the girls switched outfits, then they did the same for him.

"God it feels so good to be back in real clothes. Oh, and socks and sneakers instead of stockings!" Gillian rubbed her feet as she swapped shoes.

"Hurry up," Cole said, "We don't have time for massages."

Maggie scooped up each of their outfits and tossed them under the bed. Hope would wonder why they'd left these older clothes behind but Maggie didn't have the heart to destroy them and didn't know if they could take them back to the future. Maybe whoever had brought them in the first place would collect them.

She longed to leave a goodbye note but Maggie just didn't possess the words. On second thought, she realized if she didn't say anything, Hope would assume they'd been caught. That just wasn't fair after all her friend had been through. She had to find something to use.

Maggie rushed over to Hope's desk, reached for her diary, and ripped a page from the back of the book. She opened the drawer and dug out a small nub of pencil. She'd keep it short and simple.

Hope,

We are safe so please don't worry about us.
Keep the faith and stay sweet.

Love,
Your Friends

The sound of doors slamming drew closer. The officers had reached the second floor. *They won't find anything in Cole's room now*, Maggie sighed to herself as she placed her note on top of the diary. Nothing about her words would incriminate Hope about knowing their whereabouts. Still, it was time to set up the board and get out of there.

The Ouija board's polished wooden surface gleamed. The kids arranged themselves on Hope's quilt-covered bed.

"Everybody set?" Gillian asked.

"Not quite." Maggie shook her head and said, "Cole, I think your hands should join ours on the pointer."

"Really?" he asked.

"You've more than earned it." She smiled at her brother with a new respect.

Cole manoeuvered himself into position.

Maggie glanced around the room one last time, took a deep breath, and began. "Are you with us Hope?"

Her hands swayed back and forth with the others, the puppeteer guiding them again, until the pointer rested.

It hadn't settled on any letter or phrase.

"Now what?" Gillian cringed.

"We try again," Maggie said. "It has to work." She repeated her question, a pleading tone in her voice.

The hollering from below grew louder. She forced herself to block it out and concentrate solely on the board and the movement of her hands.

This time the pointer circled the board once and landed on

YES

Maggie felt her body sag in relief. Step one was a success. Her fingers slipped from their perch as she heard the lower attic door pulled open.

"There's no one up there," Hope said. "Those are my quarters."

"We will search them the same as the rest of this place."

"My father died for this county and my brother fights still. How dare you not believe me!" Hope shouted.

"Get out of our way!"

This was it. If it didn't work, they were done for. Maggie shivered at the thought of years in a hard labour camp. She spoke from her heart. "We love you Hope. We'll never forget this journey. Please take us home."

The words were out. All they could do now was trust that Hope's spirit would restore them to their original place and send them home before they were snatched up by the officers.

A sense of peace, intense and fulfilling, spread through Maggie. The shadowy space began to fill with a light — a light so bright and pure, once again she could no longer keep her eyes open. Maggie squeezed her lids shut but held fast to the pointer as it embarked on its path around the board.

Please say yes, she thought. Please send us home.

Maggie heard boots pound up the stairs but didn't open her eyes. The pace of the pointer intensified, spiralling then spinning around the Ouija's perimeter. It was difficult for their hands to follow the rapid movements. With her eyes firmly closed, her sense of touch heightened and somehow she managed to maintain her grip.

The pointer moved at warp speed now. The shuttered window burst open, sending a gust of air whirling through the room. Maggie continued to hang on, her hair flying from the tornado like blast. This time the kids didn't scream when the board raised itself off the floor.

Once more, Maggie felt herself floating.

Chapter Twenty-Three

As quick as it had arrived, the surge of power dissipated. Everything lay still and silent. Maggie hadn't even felt their landing. She gradually opened her eyes, blinking as they refocused. The blinding light faded and was sucked up like a pin prick into the board. As she regained her full vision, her heart leapt at the sight.

She gazed around the old attic room, once again sparse and covered in dust. They sat only on the rusty metal bed frame, the straw mattress and quilt long gone. Maggie listened for the shouts of officers but found only the sound of her breathing, then Cole's loud whoop.

Gillian grinned at her.

Cole jumped up and pumped his fists in the air. "We're home!" he cheered and raced out of the room.

"We did it," Maggie said to her friend.

"*You* did it. We were just along for the ride." Gillian smiled.

They walked out of the room arm in arm and headed downstairs. Maggie didn't look back as she closed the door.

Then from the main floor below, Cole screamed.

The girls flew down the stairs to find Cole frozen.

"What's wrong?" Maggie asked.

Cole didn't answer. He pointed at the table, the girls' hot chocolate cups still sitting half full. Maggie touched the muddy brown liquid and jerked her finger back when she found it lukewarm.

Cole turned and pointed at the clock ticking a steady beat on the kitchen wall. Four o'clock. But that was impossible … wasn't it? It couldn't be the same time as when they'd left. Maggie shook her head to rattle some common sense back into her brain.

"Cole, are you still wearing your digital watch?"

"Uh huh."

"Does it have a date display?"

Cole glanced down at his wrist, and then lifted his eyes directly in line with hers. His face transformed from fear into delight.

"It's the same day as when we left!" He jigged a happy dance around the kitchen table, grabbed Gillian, and swung her around in a circle.

"No one knows we've been gone. Mom's still at work," Maggie said, unable to believe their good fortune.

She slumped into a chair. She'd been running on adrenaline and was nearing empty.

"And I didn't miss my date with Mark tonight, 'Future Mark,'" Gillian said then gave them a menacing stare. "If either of you value your life you won't comment."

They had lots to celebrate. They were home and they were safe. Maggie wanted nothing more than to crawl into her own bed and sleep for a week, but first she needed to look around.

Instead of wandering through the rooms in a fog of grief, this time she let their warmth wrap around her. She meandered from one to the next, running her hand over family photos, smiling at the ones that included her father, and then caressed her mother's soft wool afghan, which lay folded over the arm of her reading chair.

Maggie looked briefly out the living room windows into their yard. The thunderstorm had passed but the ground remained wet. Her breath caught when she glimpsed a brilliant rainbow arching over the big oak tree.

Without thinking, she picked up the stack of mail sitting on the entry table, flipped through, not really aware of what she was reading until a name caught her eye.

She jolted wide awake.

She held a plain white envelope, addressed to a Ms. Maggie Lewis. *But I'm Maggie Kaufman*, she thought. *What's going on?*

She raced back into the kitchen as fast as her feet would carry her.

"Thank goodness you're still here," she said to Gillian. "Check this out."

"Who is she?" Gillian asked after examining the name.

"Dunno, but it's not me," Maggie said. Or was it? In spite of all they'd accomplished, she might never know what happened to Hope after they left.

"The post office is still open," Cole said. "Why don't we take it over there and see if they can help sort it out?"

"How do you know these things?" Maggie asked in disbelief.

Cole just shrugged. "What are we waiting for? Let's go."

- - -

They found Mrs. Morris, the local gossip, on postal duty when they arrived.

"You must be the Kaufman kids that just moved into the Lewis house a while back?"

The siblings nodded. *She called us Kaufman*, Maggie thought. *Phew, it's not me after all*. Her confusion remained though as the postmistress continued.

"I still slip up sometimes and call it the Morris Inn. My grandfather used to own it many years ago …"

"Do you know this person?" Maggie hated to interrupt but had a suspicion Mrs. Morris would carry on all day. She showed her the envelope.

"Maggie Lewis, oh my yes. Such a sweet thing. She's up at the retirement home on Paisley Avenue now."

"So she's still alive then?" Maggie asked.

"Slowed down some once she hit eighty, but still sharp as a tack. Why I remember …"

"Thanks, Mrs. Morris, but we gotta run." Maggie gestured to Cole and Gillian to head for the door.

"Sorry about the mix-up kids …" was all Maggie heard as they bolted down the street.

Halfway down the block, Gillian stopped. "I'd really love to join you guys on this whole senior social thing, but I can't."

Maggie understood. She'd asked more of her friend than she ever had a right to. "Go ahead and get ready for your date. Give your mom and dad a hug. Catch up with us later though?"

"You got it … and good luck."

They had to pass their house again on the way to the retirement home. Maggie and Cole stopped only long enough to pick up their bikes. She pedalled furiously and made it in minutes, her tires shuddering. Cole slammed his bike to a halt beside her, leaving black marks on the pavement.

When they asked for Ms. Lewis at the front desk, the nurse smiled at them.

"She doesn't get many visitors these days so she'll be happy to see you. Follow me."

The nurse led them down a brightly light hallway, surprisingly homey with the walls painted in warm earth tones, the shades of the fall leaves outside. Doors opened off of either side. Much to Maggie's relief, there weren't any sick people drooling in wheelchairs in the halls. Instead, it resembled an apartment complex with medical help on site.

When they reached the last door on the left, the nurse stopped and knocked.

"You have some guests, Ms. Lewis."

"Come in," a voice replied.

The nurse held the door open for them and Maggie entered first. Cole followed steps behind.

"I'll be back at the desk if you need anything," the nurse said.

"Thank you." She took a few more steps into a tiny but comfortable room, Cole following behind. Maggie had acted without thinking in coming here. She had no idea what was going to happen next or what she might face. Who was this person?

A petite woman, with steel-grey curls and pallid skin, sat in an armchair by the window, her legs covered in a warm flannel blanket. Maggie approached, drawn to the woman's eyes. They were deep blue and still full of life.

She knew in an instant whose eyes they reminded her of — Hope's.

Chapter Twenty-Four

"Hello," Ms. Lewis said in a soft voice.

"Hello." Maggie and Cole both greeted her.

"Are you selling something for school?"

"No ma'am. Just visiting. And we brought you some mail." She introduced them as she handed the envelope over. "I'm Maggie and this is my brother, Cole."

"Now that's odd. My name's Maggie too and I also have a brother named Cole."

"You do?" she asked, stunned.

As the elderly woman spoke, her voice strengthened. "My mother always spoke of her dear friend, Maggie. She named me after her. Come in and have a seat."

She motioned for the kids to sit on the couch opposite her. "She said this girl showed her the true meaning of friendship. She supported my mother through one of the most difficult times in her life."

She paused briefly, apparently recalling the memory of her mother. "She was the strongest woman I ever knew."

She passed them a plate of cookies. Cole reached for a few. Maggie couldn't believe they were actually speaking with Hope's daughter.

"My brother was named Cole after someone else my mother met. She said he reminded her of bravery and sweetness at the same time, although there were times growing up I'm sure she wondered about the sweetness part."

Maggie turned and smiled knowingly at her brother then returned her attention to Ms. Lewis. "What were your parents' names?" She needed to know who Hope had married.

"Frank and Hope Lewis."

"Your last names are Lewis?" It was a relief to know that Franz had returned. She hoped that they had shared a long and happy life together. Maggie understood how Franz could be easily changed to Frank, but why Lewis, she wondered.

She tried to calculate in her head how old Franz might be but soon realized there was no way he could still be alive. How odd that they hadn't seen his grave with the others when they'd been at the cemetery.

Maggie sidled closer to the edge of the couch and continued to listen to the old woman's words.

"My father was one of several thousand people taken into internment camps during the First World War because he was of German descent. Immigrant folks from some other countries were sent too. I heard the Ukrainians had a horrible time of it."

Ms. Lewis reached for a glass of water on the end table beside her, took a sip and continued. "Despite the fact that he'd never done anything wrong, he was ashamed of his confinement and so he changed his first name slightly and assumed my mother's surname when they got married."

We could have been right beside him in that camp, Maggie thought. If it hadn't been for Hope, she didn't even want to think about what might have happened to them. "Was he hurt at all?"

"No, just worked to the bone. But they had a good life together after that. When he passed on, my mother sprinkled his ashes under a big willow tree at the old family farm."

Maggie knew exactly which tree she meant. The same tree Hope's father's funeral had been and where she'd sat with her friend.

"And your name is Lewis too?" She still had a few questions left.

"Yes. I never married. My mother encouraged me to follow my dreams, even when it didn't bring her grandchildren. My brother helped out with that. He lives with his family down south now. I, on the other hand, wanted to travel the world. Mother even joined me on several trips. The one I remember most was when we spent two months in Europe. She was very interested in visiting some of the war memorials, as my grandfather died as a soldier over there."

Cole passed the now empty cookie plate back to Ms. Lewis. Maggie wondered about Hope's brother, Luke. Surely he survived.

"I'm sorry about your grandfather," she said.

"Thankfully we didn't lose anyone else," Ms. Lewis confirmed. "But many families weren't as fortunate."

Maggie still found it hard to comprehend the fact that it had all happened before Ms. Lewis was even born; and yet for her and the others, it had been merely days ago. She figured she'd grapple with it for a long time to come. *But there's one more thing I need to know about*, she thought.

"I think we live in your old house," Maggie said. "We just moved in a few months ago."

"That would make sense. My parents bought that place several years after they were married, when the hotel in it closed down. My mother lived there for the rest of her life. I moved in when my mother passed away. Finally, I just couldn't keep it up on my own anymore."

"We found something in your attic," Maggie said.

Cole's eyes grew wide at his sister's revelation and he gave her a swift kick. Maggie patted him on the knee and continued. "Maybe you would like to have it back … it's a Ouija board."

"You found that old thing?" Ms. Lewis tittered.

Cole eased himself back into the couch cushions.

"It was my mother's. She bought it when my brother was fighting in the Second World War. She had this crazy notion she could reach him or find out if he was safe. I thought it was ridiculous. She never confided in me whether or not she had any luck but it seemed to give her comfort."

So that's why we found it in the attic in the first place, Maggie realized. "Should we bring it to you?" she asked.

"Nah, you kids can have it. Play a game with it or something. But don't expect anything to happen … it's just a toy after all."

No way am I going to tell her, Maggie thought. Her experience with the Ouija board was staying a secret — for now at least.

As Ms. Lewis stared dreamily out her window for a moment, seemingly lost in her memories again, Maggie noticed a very familiar necklace peeking out from the collar of her blouse. She smiled and touched Hope's necklace around her own neck.

Ms. Lewis turned back to them, just as the kids rose from the couch.

"I'm sorry, but we have to get going." Maggie was anxious to see her mother and knew Cole would be as well, especially now that the cookies were eaten.

"Thank you for visiting, dear. I'm sorry if I kept you too long with my old stories."

"Not at all," Maggie said. "In fact, I'd really like to come see you again sometime, if that's okay?"

"That would be wonderful. Next time I'll have more treats." Ms. Lewis winked at Cole and rose shakily from her chair. "And some photo albums."

Overjoyed about the thought of seeing pictures of Ms. Lewis's and Hope's life, Maggie thought it would give her even more incentive to return. Not that she really needed any. She had a soft spot for the older woman already and hoped they would develop a friendship.

Ms. Lewis steadied herself with a wooden cane and walked them slowly to the door. As they were about to leave, she put a warm, wrinkled hand on Maggie's arm.

"My mother would have liked you."

"Thank you," Maggie said.

Chapter Twenty-Five

The minute the kids arrived home, Maggie crumpled onto the couch. Her sneakers dangled over the end. Her mother hated when they didn't take their shoes off but she couldn't move another muscle. Cole fell into the overstuffed armchair opposite her.

Their mother would be home within the hour but it was all she could do to stay awake. She probably wouldn't even realize they'd been gone. *Just another day of struggle for her*, Maggie thought, *and I haven't helped matters lately*.

Maggie finally gave up the fight and within seconds her eyes closed as she drifted off. The last thing she remembered was a feeling of contentment. She was finally home where she belonged.

Maggie woke to a gentle caress on her forehead. Then she realized whose hand had stroked her.

"Mom!" she cried. Her shouting woke Cole, who leapt from his chair and joined them in a crushing family hug.

"To what do I owe all of this sudden affection?" her mother asked. Her eyes watered.

"It feels like you've been gone for days," Maggie said. She wasn't ready yet to share the fact that it was actually *them* that had been gone. Maybe someday.

"I stopped at the video store and picked up some movies. I also thought I'd order some pizza ..." Her mother hesitated.

Maggie knew her mother feared her rejection, that she'd make other plans or would shut her out again. She was so sorry for causing her additional pain. While they had lost a father, their mom had lost a husband. Being angry or lashing out at anyone was not going to solve anything or help anyone. Maggie knew they needed to stick together now.

"Would you like to have a family movie night?" her mother asked.

Maggie smiled at her. The first smile she'd offered in a long time, but it came easily now. She simply said, "I'll make popcorn."

"Count me in too!" Cole cheered.

Maggie couldn't think of a better way to spend the evening. She wasn't going to set foot outside the door. It would be just the three of them. Maybe it wasn't the same as four with her dad, but it would be good. Whether it was due to their journey to the past and their experience with the Ouija board, or simply her acceptance of her grief, she wasn't sure. All she did know was she sensed her dad's presence with them now and it felt reassuring.

During the first movie, a comedy, the three of them cuddled together on the couch, fingers greasy from the buttery popcorn.

Halfway through, Gillian burst through the back door, interrupting their laughter. "Maggie! I've got to talk to you!"

Gillian's arrival wasn't unusual, this being her second home, so to speak, but she was supposed to be on her date that night — not there. The girls moved into the kitchen for some privacy.

"What's wrong?" Maggie asked.

"I broke up with Mark!"

"But I thought you really liked him?"

"Well I did, but this time travel business changed everything." Gillian plopped down on a chair, head drooped, and ran her fingers over the smooth wood table.

Maggie knew it was too good to be true that they hadn't messed up something in the time continuum. "Does this have anything to do with the Mark of the past?"

Gillian nodded but didn't look up.

"You didn't tell him about everything, did you?" Maggie wondered what people would think. Would they believe it? Would they lock them up in some loony bin thinking they were completely nuts? Put them on the evening news?

"No. I didn't tell him anything." Gillian fidgeted in her chair but Maggie knew she was telling the truth. What a relief.

"I did talk to him about his family though," Gillian continued. "And it turns out that he's related to the past Mark.... In fact it was his grandfather."

"Well what's wrong with that?" Maggie asked.

"I kissed him!"

"Which one?" Now Maggie was getting confused.

"The past Mark. I kissed his grandfather!" Gillian shuddered. "It's like creepy now or something.... I just couldn't see myself kissing both of them."

"This is just too funny." Maggie grabbed her stomach, her laughter erupting. Gillian looked at her and started laughing too. They laughed so hard they had tears in their eyes.

"Come here," Maggie finally said and gave her friend a hug. Things would be okay after all. Gillian would be on to a new guy next week, she was certain, and everything would feel normal again.

Maggie wouldn't soon forget the other side she'd seen of Gillian though. She felt like kicking herself that she'd been too wrapped up in herself to notice it sooner. She would share the hard times with her friend now too, not just the good ones. For now though, a good laugh was just what they needed.

The next morning, Maggie woke up in her own bed. When she realized where she was, she felt a renewed sense of happiness and snuggled deeper under the covers.

She floated downstairs a while later to find her mother singing in the kitchen, the smell of frying bacon making her mouth water. She ruffled Cole's already unruly mop of hair and joined them for breakfast. Another new step for her. Since her dad died, she would usually grab a muffin or piece of fruit on the run. She'd become the queen of avoidance. *Not anymore*, Maggie thought.

"Mom's going to help me make my Halloween costume tonight," Cole said, as he shoved another mouthful of scrambled eggs into his mouth.

"What are you going to be?" Maggie asked. She lathered fresh apple butter onto her toast.

"Either a time traveller or a cowboy."

"I think the cowboy would be much easier, what do you think?" Her mother said as she dried her hands on a dish-towel and joined them at the table.

"Definitely the cowboy." Maggie smiled with pride, remembering the ride back in time and her brother's bravery.

"Mom, could I get a horse?" Cole asked.

Maggie enjoyed a long hot shower, got dressed, and then stopped to say goodbye to her mom. She had something she needed to do before school.

"Would you like me to come with you?" her mother asked as she reached back into the clothes trunk, in search of the perfect costume for Cole.

"Thanks Mom. Next time I'd really like that, but today I need to go on my own."

She felt ready to start sharing her grief. Tomorrow, she'd stop by the library after school and have a nice visit with Miss Menkle. And definitely sign out some new books. No ghost stories for a while though. Maybe she'd even ask her mom to do some sort of mother-daughter book club. Books used to be her thing with her dad but it was time to start making some new traditions, and perhaps it would be a way of reaching out.

She walked down Queen Street toward Woodland Cemetery, zipping her coat up to her chin, the chilly fall breeze rustling her windbreaker. She made one quick stop on her way at the twenty-four hour super grocery's floral department.

She followed her usual path first, into the cemetery, to her father's grave.

"Thank you, Dad," Maggie said aloud. "I'm so glad we had another moment together."

She knew that she didn't need to speak the words. Her father would hear her thoughts, but it felt good to vocalize them too. She also knew that although she couldn't hear his reply with her ears, she would feel it in her heart. And she did. Her heart felt less empty.

"I may not be by as much from now on," she continued, but it wasn't an apology. "I've got some living to do and it may get busy. I know now that you'll be with me no matter where I go."

She set a pot of mums, a deep burgundy shade, in front of his tombstone and rose to her feet. "Talk to you soon," she said and walked in the direction of the older graves.

Maggie knelt in front of Hope's stone, the cool earth dampening the knees of her jeans. She placed a single pink rose, thorns and all, at the base of the precious burial marker.

"I'm sorry I never said goodbye in person." She lifted her face up to the sun and felt its heat. The warmth spread through her, as if Hope were offering her forgiveness.

"Rest in peace, my friend." Maggie reached inside her jacket and sweater. She held the wooden cross in her fingers. With her other hand, she pushed herself up to her feet. She stood in front of the stone a moment, reliving her journey in her mind. As she turned to walk away, her eyes rested on the inscription's words. She read them again slowly and grinned. A new line had appeared.

Hope Evalyn Lewis
1898–1988
Mother, Daughter, and Friend

Rest in Peace

A Life with no Regrets

Acknowledgements

The story enclosed in these pages took many years to see the light of day. Along my journey there were many who shone to help me find my way. I wish I could list them all by name. Know that if you touched my life you are never forgotten and always appreciated.

A heartfelt gratitude goes out to the following:

To Margaret Bryant for believing in this book and giving me a chance; to Jennifer McKnight for her patience and editing super powers; to Jim Hatch for his publicity prowess; and the entire talented Dundurn team. You guys rock.

To my writing colleagues everywhere, especially those who write for children and teens, you are the most supportive and encouraging group I've ever encountered, always cheering on the success of others and offering advice. Special thanks to everyone in the original Kidcrit critique group for all the lessons learned and invaluable feedback on early drafts. I wouldn't have made it this far without you.

To Charley Johnson, president of the Pay It Forward Foundation, not only for your friendship and support as I grieved and continue to heal from my mother's death, but also for sharing the Pay It Forward philosophy with me. Through kindness to others we help to heal ourselves. My fellow supporters of this movement are like family to me and are the best of the best.

To all my former library colleagues, patrons, students, and staff, I miss seeing you every day. Thanks for putting up with my neat-freak tendencies to always have the books in order on the shelves, perfectly aligned, listening to my stories, and hearing me obsess about books, books, books. Read on.

To my immediate family, relatives, and friends — especially my father, Edward Runstedler, who always encouraged my love of reading and never thought I was weird to have three books on the go at once. You always worked so hard to give us everything. My brothers, Greg and Chris, thanks for looking out for your sister and always supporting me. I know you are all surprised that I decided to be a writer. But what else would have fit?

To my beautiful daughter, Savannah — my life's greatest opus. Keep singing your song and following your dreams. You bring sunshine to every day and make me proud. I love you more than words can say.

This book is dedicated to my mother, Margaret Runstedler. She passed away before she was able to read my story, but did know that it had sold and was so excited for me. Tragically gone too soon but never ever forgotten. I hope you are reading it now and that I've made you proud. You were my biggest cheerleader, my rock, and my own beautiful goodbye.

Picturing Alyssa
by Alison Lohans
9781554889259
$12.99

Who is the girl staring out of the old photograph? Every time Alyssa Dixon looks at it, even by accident, she finds herself on an Iowa farm in 1931. The past is nothing like Alyssa's unhappy life: her mother severely depressed after the stillbirth of Alyssas baby sister; escalating bullying by Brooklynne, a popular girl; and a teacher who is unsympathetic toward Alyssas familys pacifist beliefs.

Why can't Alyssa live in the past with her new friend, Deborah? Yet Alyssa is always pulled back to the present, where things only get worse. Maybe the farm isn't so idyllic, though. Deborah's mother is ill with a difficult pregnancy, and theres so much work. A series of old family photos shows Alyssa unsettling things about Deborah's family things Deborah seems not to know. Can Alyssa help the baby be born safely, and at the same time work through the overwhelming problems at home?

Chasing the White Witch
by Marina Cohen
9781554889648
$12.99

Teased by her older brother, bullied by the popular girls at school, and plagued by a blistering pimple that has surfaced on the tip of her nose, twelve-year-old Claire Murphy wishes she could shrivel up and die or spontaneously combust. But when a mysterious book appears at her feet in the checkout aisle of a grocery store, Claire is confident all her troubles are over.

Following the instructions carefully, Claire dives nose-first into reeking remedies, rollicking rituals, and silly spells. It's only when she recklessly disregards the Law of Three that the line between good and evil blurs and Claire must race against time to undo all of the trouble she's caused.

Available at your favourite bookseller

Visit us at
Dundurn.com
@dundurnpress
Facebook.com/dundurnpress
Pinterest.com/dundurnpress

Free, downloadable Teacher Resource Guides